THE LEGACY OF LILLY GUTHRIE

BOOK I

THE
HALF LIFE

ELLIE ELISABETH

Enjoy the journey!

Ellie Elisabeth

Published by Ellie Elisabeth

ISBN 978-0-9977673-9-1

Front cover design by Stephanie Parcus
Back cover design by Luigi Gonnella

www.EllieElisabeth.com

*To you **Mom**.*
*For never giving up on **life** and*
*teaching us to always follow our **hearts**.*

"If only there were evil people somewhere insidiously committing evil deeds, and it were necessary only to separate them from the rest of us and destroy them. But the line dividing good and evil cuts through the heart of every human being. And who is willing to destroy a piece of his own heart?"

Aleksandr Solzhenitsyn

PREFACE

"The world is a dangerous place to live, not because of the people who are evil, but because of the people who don't do anything about it."

Albert Einstein

August 18, 1943

A soldier hobbled along the Sicilian countryside, dirt, or soot, or blood, it was hard to tell which, hid who he was and what was left of his uniform. His face was stone, dripping with sweat, and his thoughts only to keep going until he found anyone alive.

A groan drifted from his right. He dropped to his knee, his rifle at the ready, and scanned the vicinity. Eyes narrowed, he watched as fingers wiggled on an outstretched arm. The soldier waited, looking around again, before carefully making his way to the source of the groan.

"What's yer name, Private?" His husky voice whispered as he knelt beside the young man. He spared some water from his canteen to wet the kid's lips.

"They're coming, for me…"

"Private John Coale here. Can you stand?" There were no visible wounds on him, so John lifted him, checking his back.

"It's too late," he rasped, his hand reaching towards the sun.

7

"What's yer name? Where ye hurt?" John sighed; lowering him down, he was dead weight, cold. John brushed the soot off his own arm revealing a red cross and a green patch with a '1' on it. That's when he noticed the fresh blood on his hand.

"Private James..." he breathed, "...Ezekiel Russo. Jim. 45th..." Jim made eye contact with John for just a moment and then his eyes wandered beyond John again.

John wiped the blood on his pants, and then slid his hand in his pocket, removing a rosary. "You religious, Jim?" He took Jim's outstretched hand and held it down, placing the rosary in it.

"Look," Jim raised his other hand.

"Yea', I'm not sure anymore either." John said to himself. He lowered his head reciting, "our father who art..."

But Jim didn't hear him. The sky turned bright, as his spirit rose from his body and left John behind praying. Jim stared at his transparent, glowing, hands. In every way he was still himself, but with no physical body to weigh him down.

Floating above the battlefields, there was no longer a bloody hole in his back. And his arms, skin, everything, was clean and smooth, free of any remnants of the war. All around him more spirits ascended from their bodies.

Jim looked up from examining himself to find a massive man ten or more feet tall wearing a gray tunic, golden chainmail, and sandals with leather straps that climbed up his calves. His legs and arms were bound with tattoos of ancient symbols and runes. At his side rested a sword as long as Jim was tall.

"You're here," Jim gulped, "for me?"

"You believe in your heart you belong elsewhere." The man stated flatly.

"Look what we've done," Jim motioned.

The man nodded solemnly and placed his hand on Jim's shoulder. All around them turned bright white and great white wings appeared behind the man Jim now knew as an angel.

But darkness grew around them and they were forced to a stop. "He's right you know, he doesn't deserve to go with you, Raziel," growled a voice.

"Azazel." Raziel's voice was flat.

Azazel's wings were like a dying dragon's and all that showed behind his cloak were two red eyes and outlines of a weak bony face. Azazel reached out and grabbed for Jim. As Azazel touched Jim, lightning and thunder cracked through the sky and both Raziel and Azazel were thrown backward from Jim's spirit.

John continued to pray over Jim's body, unaware of the battle for Jim's soul.

Azazel snapped and snarled at Raziel, but Raziel smiled.

Both angel and demon lunged for Jim. All around him became a haze of dark shadow and blue light. It was unclear where one began and the other ended, even Jim himself was impossible to define. Neither Azazel or Raziel could draw their swords or call for help from the others; they were only able to struggle against one another's force.

Finally they threw themselves apart and scattered between them was a mess of dim blue light, what was left of Jim. Raziel lowered his hand to rest on the hilt of his sword.

"Silly angel," Azazel cackled.

"PAX!" Raziel shouted as he threw his hand out.

A glowing force hit Azazel by surprise, knocking him over. Azazel jumped up, extending his own arm, "PAX!"

A force whizzed through the air hitting Raziel, but he was prepared and barely budged.

The shadow and light met at Jim's dwindling spirit, tossing it around in the air. Jim's spirit cried out in pain trying to escape, but he couldn't push free.

Azazel laughed at Jim's cries, leaving Raziel sullen. Yet, Raziel never considering ceasing and letting Azazel win.

Both their forces threw them back again, exhausted and unable to continue. They watched as the dark and light continued to speed around Jim, circling so quickly his spirit couldn't be seen.

Suddenly, Jim's screams stopped and the light and dark were gone. A fog fell away, revealing Jim in a new flawless body. He threw his head back and cried out. Out came a darkness that jolted back to Azazel and a light that sped back to Raziel. Jim fell to the ground.

John looked up from his prayer over Jim's old, lifeless body. The renewed Jim sat before him naked, clean, with bright-untarnished skin and clean shaggy black hair. He crouched over, heaving for air, but breathing didn't feel like breathing anymore. It was harsh and unnecessary; still he sucked in more and more air trying to breathe, fearing he would die without it.

Azazel cackled.

"Jim?" John stood pale, eyes darting back and forth between the twin bodies.

"It's Zeke now," Azazel hissed, allowing John to see him for a brief moment, which was enough to send John running.

Azazel licked his lips and paced towards *Zeke*.

11

Raziel placed his hand on Zeke and plain clothes appeared on his body.

Stopping, Azazel craned his neck as if he heard something. "Next time," he uttered; with one sweep of his leathery wings he was fifty feet up. Turning sharply, he sped directly at the ground, but before he hit, the ground turned to fire and Azazel disappeared into a molten ash.

"Hide yourself from them, before you scare more." Raziel motioned towards the sea of human bodies, mostly dead, but some still living.

"What? How? What am I?" Zeke replied in shocked.

"You are a *Half Life*; the product of *Pax*, the kiss of death. Your soul was undecided, you must live equally as human, angel, and demon until *you* resolve where you belong."

Zeke's red-eyed gaze stared up at the angel.

"Think 'lateo.'" Raziel ignored Zeke's anger.

Zeke thought, *lateo* and everything around him changed. The battlefield went dark, black-cloaked demons with scales and red eyes darted in and out of sight, snatching souls from their bodies. A few angels could be seen fighting for souls, shouting *Pax,* as Raziel did, but mostly there were the others, the demons.

"When you don't want to be seen, just think *lateo* and you'll be hidden."

"And I'll come here?"

"Yes, this is Abditus." Raziel saw Zeke's disappointment. "I am sorry. I tried my best to take you home."

Zeke stared at him bitterly, then thought of his own home, and disappeared.

CHAPTER 1

"A woman would rather visit her own grave than the place where she has been young and beautiful after she is aged and ugly."

Thomas Hardy

Modern Day

Zeke leaned back on his elbows and stretched himself out over the bleachers. A cigarette rested behind his right ear, nearly hidden by dark brown hair. He kicked his Alden boots up on the railing and leaned forward to fix the roll in his jeans. The wind blew so powerfully, his leather jacket swept away from his chest, revealing a pack of Camels tucked inside his jacket and his dog tags, leaving only a thin white undershirt to protect him from the cold. But Zeke didn't notice, he simply leaned back and looked up.

"C'mon'." Zeke said.

The clouds hovered like curtains in the sky, blocking any chance of seeing the stars, and sweeping the moon in and out of hiding. A few shoddy florescent lights up at the school buzzed; they were intended to discourage vandalism. The graffiti proved them worthless. They flickered and the wind stopped. Nature itself stood still.

Abruptly, the wind gust harshly in the opposite direction it had been, making Zeke's dog tags clink. As if the wind spoke to him, Zeke shot upright and stared into the dark football field. If there was something to see, it couldn't be seen, but he was sure he had just received his signal. *She* was here.

He made his way under the bleachers and pulled a note form his pocket.

Football Field, Midnight.

The paper was torn around all the edges, clearly ripped from one of Zeke's notebooks. He still hadn't figured out which one. Someone going through his things while he slept bugged him, but there was no getting past it in a world like this.

"You can come out now. You've made me wait long enough," Zeke droned, looking around under the bleachers.

He slid the cigarette out from behind his ear, brushing back his hair and placed it firmly between his lips. Flipping his lighter open he lit it and took a drag. He lit the strip of paper next.

"Never in control," he murmured, infatuated by the flame burning the paper. It curled and singed black over the letters written across it, the words turning to ash and gliding to the earth. He slid the lighter back into his pants pocket.

They didn't leave a name, but judging by the sloppy handwriting, he knew who wrote it. He knew who placed it on his chest while he slept, just to taunt him. There was little Gahdarina could say to convince him to do business with her again. But he could not ignore a call, that was the rule. Angel or demon, a Half Life could not ignore a call, at least not without consequences. It was all part of the game, part of his pitiful existence; he had to at least hear her out, even if he would be happy never seeing her face again.

The other side, the angels, always wrote in elegant flowing cursive. But they never dealt with him anymore, at least not through notes that led him to Wakefield High at midnight.

No, he thought as the red of the flame burned in his eyes; *this is my side. The demons.* Still, he wouldn't take the job, not now, not when school just started back up. He needed time to think and enjoy being a teenager *again*. It was better than his pervious posts at the law firm, political events, airport duty, and Iowa (he still could not figure out, why Iowa?) put together. Teenagers were easy to influence, and despite their hormones and attitudes, they were spontaneous and free in a way adults could never be. Besides he liked having a home with his mentor, Skoal.

The fire interrupted his thoughts as it turned his fingernails black. The burning paper slipped from his hand and fell to the earth, dying out halfway down. He wiped the soot on his white shirt, leaving dark steaks down it.

Zeke crossed his arms and stared at the solid earth. "I'm still waiting." Smoke escaped from his mouth as he spoke.

A mini cyclone came rushing up from the ground, air pushing at him from all sides. Zeke felt it crushing his chest, tossing the cigarette from his mouth. He backed out from under the bleachers to where the air was calm.

It stopped and silence ate away at the night. The bits of grass, earth, and leaves that had been swirled around now lay in a circle under the bleachers. Zeke, lighting another cigarette, stared at the center, knowing all too well what would happen next.

There came a low hissing and then popping sounds like cracking knuckles. The lights around the school shut off completely and a green fiery glow appeared emanating from *beneath* the earth. A dark cloaked figure slowly rose straight up from the circle of debris, producing the burning smell of sulfur and a terrible cackling.

A hood covered the figure's face. If it weren't for the green fire that burned in a circle around her feet, the creature would have been completely void of light. Her hands were young and beautiful in the glow as they rose to brush the hood of her cloak back.

She had short black and silver hair. Her nose was sharp and her lips greedy as they stretched coercively about her face. By far, the worst part of her were the eyes, cold and careless, yet vindictive, bright red eyes. The fiery light glistened over her pale skin, her beauty making her seem peerless.

"Oh, my dear Zeke, I didn't scare you did I?" She grinned.

Zeke grunted. "No, Gahd. I'm used to your unnecessary theatrics." He turned his back to her and stalked off.

"Wait!" She croaked, reaching out to him.

Desperate. Zeke smiled. He paused, back still to her.

Gahd's hand clutched his shoulder and in the moonlight her fingers were wrinkled, old, and leathery. The moon was determined to expose her true nature. It was a blessing demons were exposed at night, but a curse that the sun hid their true nature.

Zeke craned his neck and swiped her skeleton of a hand away in disgust.

Gahd scoffed at his distaste.

"What?" He laughed, almost as nastily as she had.

She was gazing at her now beautiful human fingers, illuminated by her own fiery glow. When she looked up again, Zeke was smoking, staring up at the clouds.

"I have a new contract for you," she said.

"I'm not interested."

"You have to read it before you entirely discredit it." She wisped a scroll from her cloak and let it unravel in front of him. "You'll have a visitor soon."

Clutching the warm cigarette between his lips, Zeke sucked in and then released, still staring away.

"Just read it."

Zeke turned and snatched the scroll from her. His eyes ran quickly over line after line. "What makes her so important?" He paused, reading on. "And the Ferryman, that's a myth? If not, it would be against the rules to tell her about something of *our* world."

Gahd stepped behind him. "That's not part of *your* contract. You influence them, damn them, we do the rest." Her hand brushed his cheek. "These things will kill you." She grasped his cigarette and put it out with her fingertips.

"I wish..." Zeke mumbled as he slid another one from the pack and placed it behind his ear. He brushed his fingers over the last few words of the contract:

...Final contract for contracted, Zeke North.

19

"Final?" Zeke whispered.

"*Final.*"

Zeke stared at the contract for a long time thinking of the possibilities, of what final meant for him. He would no longer be half in, half out. No more teetering between life and death. Never again human, just Zeke. Just damned, Zeke.

"No." He threw the scroll at her. "Skoal wouldn't want me doing this. Not yet."

"Skoal!" She hissed in disapproval, her red eyes blazing. "Who cares what Skoal thinks? This is about you."

Zeke chewed his cheek in thought. "This could be it."

"Yes." That nauseating smile crept over her mouth again.

"No, Gahd." Zeke pushed away from her.

"Gahdarina," she growled, as Zeke marched away.

Before he got far she grasped his shoulder, turned him, and pulled him in close. With all his strength Zeke couldn't pull away. Despite a few benefits, a Half Life was still no match for a demon in strength. Her hands firmly on his shoulders, she smiled and brought her lips within the warmth of his.

He raised his lips over bared teeth, nostrils flaring. "Try another angle."

Gahd shrugged, dropping her grip. As she turned, her scaly red wings extended over her shoulders, ready to fly. "You always make this process so difficult. All I need is your... signature." She smiled over her wings at him, contract in hand.

"It's what you need it for that concerns me."

"You will sign, Zeke," her voice commanded, "we both know that," she circled round him, "because you've always been one of us. You dance that fine red line, but we both know where you belong. One more contract and you will be a powerful demon." She dropped the contract in his hands.

Staring at the foul handwriting on the contract, Zeke rubbed the paper between his fingers. Just paper, only words, but somehow binding.

"Demon to be," he said and thrust his hand down the side of the contract, thoroughly slicing his hand open, finger to palm. He smiled at the blood dripping down his hand, and smudged his mutilated hand over the bottom of the contract.

Without a word, Gahd snatched the scroll from Zeke, rolled it up under her cloak, and disappeared right before his eyes. Her greedy smile lingered behind.

All she wanted was blood. He chewed his cheek and stared at his inept bloody human hand. Watching the blood, feeling the pain it caused, made him feel alive again, if only for a moment. It dripped, dripped, dripped, and as he stared the cut closed up, perfectly healed as if it had never happened. He wiped the blood carelessly on his shirt as he stepped out from under the bleachers. His brand new undershirt was now tainted with a smeared red handprint and ash.

The wind had calmed and the clouds dissipated with it, allowing the stars to glisten freely.

Freely, thought Zeke with a mocking grunt. As he made his way to his car he couldn't help thinking why it was so important to Gahd that he took this contract.

And what was so special about the girl?

CHAPTER 2

"Injustice in the end produces independence."

Voltaire

"Lilly," a raspy voice murmured.

The bedroom door cracked open and a small girl with green eyes and long red hair cautiously stepped in.

"Go back to bed, Emma. It's too early." Lilly nudged Emma towards the doorway, pretending to yawn.

"The sun's up and *you're* dressed." Emma rubbed her dusty eyes.

"I'm 'bout to pass out, just had to pee, kid."

"You slept in your clothes?" Emma stared up at her sister.

If Emma was short for her age, Lilly was tall. The volleyball team had begged Lilly to play, but she brushed them off. She preferred basketball or softball and as a natural athlete, she could be picky with sports.

Lilly knelt down to Emma. "As usual. Now go back to bed for like... two hours and I'll make you breakfast."

"Pancakes?" Emma's eyes lit up.

Lilly nodded. At that Emma shuffled down the hall to her bedroom and shut the door, slowly. Lilly carefully left her own door cracked just slightly. Pacing back towards her dresser, she stepped back and forth over the old wood floorboards, searching for the loose one.

Her room was filled with grand antique furniture, all dark stained wood, no knick-knacks or books, just the frame of a perfect room. Floral wallpaper peeked out from behind the Victorian headboard, side tables, and a peculiar gothic mirror. Lilly could easily remember picking out each piece of furniture with her mother, Eva. The only personal touch to the room was a lone poster of the Northern Lights near the doorway.

One of the floorboards creaked just right. She knelt down and pulled up the board, making sure not to break it. She reached below the floor and pulled out a 1995 Wakefield High yearbook and a rosewood box with detailed wings carved into it. She took a key from her pocket and used it to open the box. Inside sat stacks of cash, a large rectangular locket with a wunjo rune, " ᚹ ", on it, and a note that simply read:

" *Lilly, your mother went to Wakefield. You should, too.* "

Once more she read over the note as she sat the box on the bed. Neatly folded at the end of the bed was a large faded yellow and blue crocheted blanket that lay atop a thick stitched quilt. She brushed her hand back and forth over the stitches of the quilt wondering who left the note and money, and why?

Lilly took the locket from the box, replacing it with the note, then shut and locked the box again. She opened the locket and placed the small key to the box inside next to a second key, shut it, and hung it safely around her neck.

The only photo in the room rested on the bedside table. Lilly touched it lightly, tipping it over. Her mother's face stared back at her from the photo.

"Mom," Lilly whispered.

She pressed her hand down against the stitching of the quilt. When she pulled her hand away the diamond stitches were etched into her hand. As she stared at her hand she found herself staring at her hand as a child.

As young Lilly sat in anticipation, diamonds etched into the palms of her hands from her quilt. "...Matthew, Mark, Luke, and John, God bless the bed that I lie on. Four corners to my bed. Four angels 'round my head. One to watch, one to pray, and two to keep my soul 'til day." Her mom, Eva, sang. She kissed Lilly's forehead, then as she stood at the door, she looked back at Lilly before leaving. The moonlight bounced off her pale skin and her blue eyes twinkled.

Lilly shook her head. That was it, there was nothing left for her to remember about Adrian, Michigan, and if there was, it had long been forgotten.

Taking the photo from the bedside table and a pair of shoes from the floor, she placed them at the top of the last moving box, along with the rosewood box.

Rays of light shone in through the break in the curtains; the sun was rising. She flipped the light switch off, snagged the box, and closed the door to her bedroom as quietly as she could. The rest of the house was much like her room: full of antique furniture, but stripped clean of any personal belongings.

Stepping down the hall Lilly glanced to Emma's room.

"She's fine." Her eyes darted away and she dashed down the steps.

Next to the front door sat a table for mail with family photos hanging on the wall above it. Lilly snagged one of the five of them. Lilly's parents beamed in the photo, as did their three children. Vincent, the oldest, had black hair and was very tall and slender. Lilly and Vincent's eyes and smiles matched their mother's. Emma's red hair and facial features mostly resembled their dad.

She sat the photo in the box as she left and shut the door gently behind her. After locking the door, Lilly took an envelope from the box. The note to Lilly's father, Simon, gave him her new address and said goodbye, but nothing too elaborate.

Lilly taped the letter to the front door, running her fingers over the tape again and again, making sure it stuck. Or maybe she was delaying, giving herself a chance for second thoughts. Nevertheless, she let the screen door go.

Starting her Sunfire, the engine roared to life, helping her ignore the tiny thought in the back of her head telling her to stay. No, Lilly Guthrie was done with that oversized, grossly yellow colonial and on her way to Wakefield, Maryland.

CHAPTER 3

"The courage of many people will falter because of the fearful fate they see coming upon the earth, for the stability of the very heavens will be broken up."

Luke 21:26

The pain in Zeke's hand was no longer apparent as he quietly stepped into the house he shared with his mentor, Skoal, and fellow Half Life, Jaymie. Zeke hated doing normal things like opening doors, when he could silently slip into his bedroom without Skoal even knowing. But he was upset right now, too human to Fade—what the supernatural world called teleporting through Abditus. Besides, Skoal chastised Zeke and Jaymie for doing things as the angels and demons did, warning them that they were human first and supernatural second, which is likely why Jaymie was rarely around.

Zeke slid the door shut behind him.

He had spent the early hours of the morning pacing the school, thinking about Gahd's contract and repeatedly imagining the pain in his hand. Zeke slid the door shut behind him gently.

"Oh, Zeke, you're home," Skoal called.

Zeke cursed to himself.

"Have you heard? Sybil, the Oracle, has gone missing. Very strange, last night in fact. Seymour has gone into hiding."

Skoal almost always wore a suit. Today's three piece was olive with a light brown tie. His hair was very short on the sides and what was left on top was slicked back. A thin mustache and strip of chin hair rested on his dark square face. Skoal didn't try to look intimidating, he simply held looking good and being confident in high regard.

Zeke dragged his feet into the kitchen where Skoal was. He had the table covered in roses and daggers: black, red, white. In one hand he held open a tattered book, his other hand was extended, palm down, with fingers sprawled, clutching the air, willing the objects to move.

"Where have you been? Not skipping school again, I hope. It's been days..." He raised his hand and obediently two daggers and one rose followed upward, while the black roses disappeared altogether.

Skoal was a Manipulator. Some might call it magic, but it's simpler than that. Manipulation is about bending time and space, not illusions or wands. Anyone could do it if their mind was open to it. Roughly three hundred years ago Skoal had been taught the secret to using the depths of his mind and the Manipulator abilities had been pouring out ever since.

29

Slinking into a chair at the table, Zeke stared at his blood-crusted hand. He made a fist, cracking the blood that coated it. He hadn't noticed Skoal's words, he was concentrating on Gahd's.

"She was so confident I would sign..." Zeke whispered, a flake of dried blood falling next to one of the white roses.

"What is that? On your hand. Zeke? Is that... blood?" Skoal's voice wavered, observing the blood and knowing all too well what a Half Life's blood was used for. The objects hovering above the table began to shake.

"Gahdarina." Zeke lowered his head.

Skoal's hand dropped. The rose fell and crossed stems with another, and the tips of the daggers struck the table, leaving them vertical.

"I shouldn't have...I'm not ready... I don't know if it's really what I want." Zeke spoke to himself.

"What have you done? Do you listen to anything I say?" With Skoal's anger the roses turned to flame, then ash.

"She said she knew I would sign." Zeke's voice shook.

"It's not that she knows Zeke, it's not about fate! She only uses it as a tactic to get you to sign. You and you alone control your actions." Skoal's hand crashed down onto the table, shaking all its contents.

"I don't want to argue about fate and will with you Skoal. The contract..."

"What is the contract? She said it would be your last, didn't she?"

Zeke didn't respond. He looked down, struggling with his thoughts. He was free from the life of a human and the petty rules of parental guidance, yet Skoal acted more like a parent than his own ever had.

"It's my life. I make my own decisions, Skoal. Some are going to bad decisions, Gahd proves that."

"After all this time, you damn yourself and blame it on Gahd? It's simple, say no, don't sign-"

"Stop! I'll fix it!" Zeke stood. "I'll find the contract-"

"Don't be a fool Zeke! You know just as well as I do, your word is hers now, your blood is hers! She'll know if you break one task of that contract. And you know what happens if you break your word."

"Torture for eternity..." Sinking back down into the chair, Zeke nodded. He knew, of course, that demons didn't waste time. The miserable creatures ingested every signed contract to insure they were carried out. Gahd would *feel* his every move.

"I wished I'd ripped it up right in front of Gahd." He looked up at Skoal, who was finally calm. "But knowing her, she probably had a spare on her...A final contract was so tempting; I could be a real demon. Fight for the underworld, where I belong."

Skoal opened his mouth to speak, but Zeke motioned for him to stop.

"Is it so wrong? I get along with the Gahds and Azazels of our world. They are *living* too, they deserve better than Hell. That's all they're fighting for."

Skoal paused. "No one is perfect Zeke, but that doesn't mean you're damned. Everyone in their right mind knows in the simplest of terms that the underworld is not the place you want to be. Don't do this to yourself."

"What choice do I have now? I'm destined--demon to be."

Skoal rested his hand on Zeke's shoulder.

"Right and wrong does not always correlate to good and evil. A wrong turn doesn't always take you to the wrong place."

They remained in silence, only hearing their own breath and cars passing by outside. Despite his intensity, Skoal knew that if he was calm, that energy would circulate to Zeke, a talent that only worked when Zeke was acting as a bull-headed human.

"Skoal... there's something off about the contract."

Skoal waited.

"A girl. Tuesday is her first day at Wakefield."

"And she's the contract?"

"Yes. I--I have to test her. The way it's written, it's not like normal contracts where I just influence someone and it's done. Or when Gahd has me make each influence a bigger task... It's written as if they know she can't be influenced at all and I try again and again. Who couldn't be influenced at all, Skoal? What kind of person is that?"

Skoal crossed one hand under his chin, half covering his mouth.

"I'm supposed to ask her about the sword, the Ferryman, which I thought was a myth, but if it's real, I mean that's like telling her what a Half Life is. It's against every rule. Then, I damn her."

Skoal stood completely motionless. "Follow the contract to a T." He paused. "Visit your friend Samael. See if he knows anything about this or Sybil's disappearance. It's no coincidence; they have to be related. I'll find what I can about the sword."

With that, Skoal disappeared before his eyes, Faded into the next room. He loved showing off his Manipulator talents; Zeke simply shook his head, as Half Lives were essentially natural Manipulators. Skoal searched his books for those on the Ferryman.

Part of Zeke that died decades ago was still in him, he couldn't get rid of it. The twenty year old that only listened to himself and his impulsive feelings coaxed Zeke to be reckless.

Zeke Faded. He stood outside a little farmhouse covered in vines.

CHAPTER 4

"There might be some hours of loneliness. But there was something wonderful even in loneliness. At least you belonged to yourself when you were lonely."

L.M. Montgomery, Mistress Pat

By three o'clock, the dotted white lines between the lanes were blurring into one endless line down the highway. Every town looked just like the last—a few trees, houses, restaurants, and gas stations. She slapped her own cheek and drew her eyes wide to stay awake, checking each sign for a decent rest stop to stretch and eat.

A familiar rock song played from her cell phone. Carefully, Lilly reached onto the passenger seat for it.

"Vin." Her lip curled.

She put the phone on speaker and sat the phone in the center console. "Hello."

"Hey Lil, whatcha up to today?" Vin asked cheerily.

"Just taking a joyride, can I call you later?"

"Lilly, where are you?" His voice was harsh now.

"Honestly Vin, why does it matter? Where are you? Across the country. It doesn't matter where I am."

"Emma left me a voicemail crying this morning, I just finally got back to her-"

"It's three o'clock Vin, I left at seven, and you're just calling me? Seriously?" Lilly took the next exit. Her face was red and her hands clenched the steering wheel.

"I have responsibilities at UCLA, I can't just drop everything because you ran off. I'll be home in a year or two. But you just leaving Emma like that, that's not ok."

"Dad knew."

"Are you insane, how would he know? Did you tell him? Did you tell anyone?"

"No, but he must have signed my transfer papers."

"Then why didn't he tell us? You have to communicate, Lilly!"

"Probably because you're too busy trying to cure cancer to bother with your family that's still here." Lilly ended the call. "Jerk."

She sped off the exit to Gettysburg and followed the signs to the nearest fast food joint. The roads were lined with carved wooden barriers, chevaux de frise, worn down houses, and cannons.

As soon as she pulled into the parking lot of a fast food place, her phone rang again. She closed her eyes and took a few deep breaths before answering. "Vincent."

"Where are you, Lilly?"

36

Lilly didn't answer; she shut her eyes and took a deep breath, counting to ten in her head.

"You're in Wakefield, aren't you?" Vincent accused.

"So?"

"What good is goin' to mom's old high school gonna do? It won't bring her back, Lil."

"Neither will curing cancer. At least I can get to know who she was." Lilly considered telling him about the note, but thought better of it.

"I have to go." Lilly took her purse and got out of the car.

"Consider going home."

"No."

"Then be careful."

This time Vincent hung up.

She put her phone in her purse and locked the car. Stretching her legs, she tried to push Vincent from her head.

This was her chance to start new, Lilly thought as she walked up to the fast food restaurant. Reaching for the door, a man grabbed it first and held it open for her. Slowly, Lilly turned to see a man with crooked yellow teeth smiling down at her. He was well over six feet tall, reeked of cigarettes, and looked at her expectantly.

At first glance, Lilly thought his eyes were red, but before she was able to take a closer look a familiar pain throbbed through her wrists. It felt like her wrists were being cut open. She held them, hoping the pressure would subdue the pain and hustled through the door without a hint of a "thank you" to him. Staring down, holding her wrist, she rushed to the bathroom.

There was no window in the single bathroom and the floor, of course, was coated with some sort of liquid. One could only hope that at least the majority of it was water as it squelched under her shoes, but its sticky consistency begged to differ.

Lilly gazed in the dirty mirror at herself. There were wide blackened bags under her bloodshot eyes. Her hair was falling out of the bun it was in, and she realized that she had put her shirt on backwards.

"Wow." Lilly scrubbed her face. "At least I've got time to waste," she said to herself, wanting to avoid the creepy man.

It was a wonder he even looked at her, considering the mess that she was, leaving her wondering what kind of people lived in Gettysburg. Leisurely, Lilly turned her shirt around and grudgingly fixed her bun. Even if she had been driving for hours, looking half-crazy in public put her off.

After glancing over her hair a few times and straightening her shirt, Lilly decided she couldn't wait any longer. The door handle had jiggled a few times and it was easy to imagine a little girl on the other side dancing around on her tiptoes.

The door skid opened and as Lilly suspected it was a little girl, who looked very relieved that Lilly was done. She held the door open and the little girl dashed in. As she got in line, Lilly noticed the girl's mother watching, her eyes intent on the door, waiting for it to open again. Lilly remembered that look.

When she was little, Lilly got lost in the mall. She stopped to watch a clown making balloon animals and by the time she looked back, her parents were gone. She found herself leaning against the second floor railing, alone in a crowded mall. There was a man that day too, who stared at her in the same eerie way. After looking around, he paced towards her. The same pain rose in her wrists, but it was less familiar to her then.

But before the man got to young Lilly, someone passed by and took her by the hand. The pains immediately stopped and her savior hid her. When she tried to look up at the face of the person who undoubtedly saved her from being kidnapped, the person was gone. Vanished without a word. The next thing she knew her parents were scolding her for wandering off.

Strange things were always happening to Lilly.

There were only a few people ahead of her in line when she realized she hadn't spent enough time dilly-dallying. The creepy man was sitting down eating his food, staring right at her.

Despite avoiding eye contact with him, she still felt his stare as she fidgeted in line. It was like sitting in the front of the classroom and being called on by the teacher and feeling her classmates staring. Lilly's heart pounded, a little scared, but mostly angry.

"Why me…" Lilly whispered.

"Can I take your order?" the cashier asked.

She looked up from her daze. The cashier stared, his fingers curling around the register anxiously.

"Your order," he grunted.

"Number seven, to go. Water."

She handed him cash and glanced behind her, unable to take the feeling anymore, needing to know if the man was still watching. Sure enough, he was. His food was gone and he stood, still staring at her. Lilly took a sharp breath in and snapped her head back to the counter. The cashier was holding out change and her food was on the counter. Lilly grabbed the bag and headed for the door, leaving the change.

"Miss, your change!"

Her feet were nearing a run as she made her way to the door. People stared, confused by her outburst. The man was following, only a few feet away now, but no one seemed to notice his strange behavior, only hers.

Why is he doing this? Lilly thought in anger.

There were so many people around, someone would notice. But notice what? What were his intentions?

Lilly pushed the door open so hard it slammed against the outside wall. Dashing to her car, she didn't dare take the time to close her jacket as she hit the cold outside air. As she jumped in her car, he was standing at the restaurant doors, glaring at her.

Lilly tore out of the parking lot, sure she saw red in his eyes this time.

A nasty grin spread across the man's face. He seemed more content now, as if he had just wanted to scare her.

The pains in her wrists subsided. It came and went as it pleased, making Lilly wonder what was wrong with her. A few years ago she had complained so much about it her dad took her to the doctor. After hours in the waiting room and X-rays, they figured it out! There was nothing wrong. Other than the thin scars on the sides of her wrists, which everyone swore they knew nothing about, her wrists were normal. They told her she was having growing pains, but Lilly knew they weren't. But with no way to medically treat it Lilly tried to ignore it, never mentioning it again, so they wouldn't start testing her head next.

Pop, pop, pop.

Rain came down as she pulled off in Wakefield.

'Wakefield High: Continuing Excellence' she read through the wipers as she slowed down. The rain picked up, coming down like bullets, pelting the windshield. It looked more like a prep school than the public school it actually was, with its perfectly trimmed bushes and ribbon awards displayed on the school. Lilly pictured the students standing in single file lines and moving around mechanically, like robots.

Lilly laughed to herself and shook her head at the thought.

A crowd of people rushed to their cars from the football field. Boys in tight black padded pants and cleats carried their shoulder pads with red uniforms draped over them. They were soaked and muddy from head to toe, giving the impression it had been raining in Wakefield a lot longer than Lilly knew.

Most of their faces were indistinguishable, but there was one face that caught Lilly's eye. Through the raindrops and windshield wipers, a kid leaned against the wall of the school. His hair was slicked back, dripping with rain. He wore a black shirt and leather jacket, the kind they wore in the fifties, at least it looked like the ones greasers wore in the movies. He exchanged something with a blonde haired kid.

The boy's head jolted in Lilly's direction. She couldn't make out his face exactly in the rain, but she could feel the way he was looking at her, like the guy in the fast food place, like there was something about her to question and—

HONK! The car behind her beeped.

Surprised, she tried to gun it and wound up hydroplaning on the water-strewn street. She waited, then eased on the gas.

It was dark out by the time she left the leasing office and pulled up at her apartment. After grabbing a few essential items-- her purse, a pillow, the wooden box, and a sleeping bag from the car--she headed inside through the rain, to her top floor apartment.

The walls were all the same color throughout, a plain off-white, and the carpet was so new it felt like walking on a cloud. Lilly took off her shoes and walked across the light brown carpet that accented the walls, both saying, 'I dare you to stain me.'

Gazing into the kitchen, she wondered where she could safely hide the wooden box filled with cash. She pushed the box into the back of the bottom corner cabinet, back where she could barely see or reach it. She closed the cabinet, content.

Staring across the apartment, her heart fluttered. Lilly felt truly alone for the first time in her life. Not the kind of overwhelming alone she felt when her mom died. That was an alone she had brushed off as soon as possible because that alone bore painful *gifts*. Or the alone she felt with her family, because she knew they didn't understand her.

This alone was scarier. It burned Lilly's throat, but she tore it back. She wasn't about to let herself get caught up in childish emotions about being away from home. She was going to enjoy this alone, where no one could bug her in Wakefield.

That's the best part of this, Lilly thought. "Being alone." Her voice echoed through the empty apartment.

Growing up, everyone knew her as the kid with the crazy mother that babbled about demons trying to kill her. Their whispers that she was better off without her crazy mother still made her angry. Lilly ground her teeth at the thought of Adrian.

Across the hall the bedroom door hung open, revealing its emptiness. "No bed, no bedroom."

Lilly dropped her pillow in the middle of the living room and laid out the sleeping bag. She burrowed into the sleeping bag and snagged her iPod and headphones from her purse.

"My new life," she murmured.

Slipping the ear buds in, Lilly hit play and a familiar song hummed in her ears as she dozed off.

CHAPTER 5

"To act from pure benevolence is not possible for finite human beings. Human benevolence is mingled with vanity, interest, or some other motive."

Samuel Johnson

Lilly woke the next morning stiff, cranky, and far too early. She lay there a few minutes, contenting herself that she had both today and Monday (for some teacher development day) off to get settled into Wakefield.

The sun was glaring in at Lilly, daring her to sleep longer. It was easy to forget what things looked like in the light, allowing her to leave the shades up the night before. The thermostat had also been overlooked. Lilly shivered, realizing she needed to turn on the heat.

Looking out the window, she groaned, "being an adult stinks." She laid her head back on the pillow and curled up in the sleeping bag. Her iPod read 6:45. Lilly groaned again as she stood and stretched.

"Dear pillow, I miss you already."

Her stomach grumbled. Responsibility lingered; a job, food, and preparations for her first day at Wakefield High.

Combing her fingers through her hair and pulling it back into a loose ponytail, Lilly left the apartment still wearing the clothes from the previous day's trip. Her car was filled with everything she needed for day-to-day life and a few things she couldn't bear to leave in that place she had once called home.

Yet, there still wasn't any furniture. There was nowhere for her clothes to go and she wasn't sure how many more nights she could spend on the floor. But she would deal with it for now; she would rather none at all than furniture from back home.

"I can find a cheap mattress somewhere," she yawned.

When she first started planning, she had decided that the money she found in her room was start-up and emergency money only. She had a bit of savings in the bank, but she had to get a job for the cost of living or she'd go broke and end up back in Adrian before the school year was out.

The dusty box filled with cash, key, and note had left Lilly conflicted when she had first stumbled--literally--on the old floorboard. The awkward thought that someone, unknown to Lilly, knew her *and* her mother, gave her hope they could tell her about her mom. Talking about Mom was something her father, Simon, seemed incapable of doing and her mom had no friends or family that Lilly knew of. Nevertheless, Lilly hoped she would come to know that peculiar someone who left her money and a mission.

The first box Lilly grabbed from the car had her toiletries, candles, and a few beauty products. Once back at the door of the apartments, Lilly leaned the box between her leg and the wall beside the door so she could get the keys out of her pocket. The box slipped and she rushed to grab it only to drop the keys on the ground. Exasperated, she threw her head back with her eyes clenched shut and groaned.

"That good of a day, already?" a man's voice chuckled.

Startled by the unexpected voice, she jumped and the box fell from her hands. Before it was able to hit the ground the man snatched it in such a smooth motion it looked rehearsed. The box wasn't on the ground, but it was no longer in Lilly's possession. Her eyes narrowed as she looked him over.

He was quite tall, and his muscles were apparent even through the layered workout gear. Physically he was in such good shape Lilly couldn't estimate his age. If someone merely saw the size of him they would quickly choose not to pick a fight.

But his face was a different story. Not a thing about his looks would change his welcoming presence. He had a very distinct jaw line, and blue, no maybe green, eyes. As their eyes met, Lilly's mind cleared and she breathed evenly.

In his left hand was the box she had nearly dropped twice. In his right hand he loosely held two leashes attached to dogs who clearly didn't need them. Both dogs sat calmly at his feet wagging their tails, and tilting their heads as if they were curiously smiling as well. One was around two feet high at the shoulders, with an oddly shaped head, thin body, and dark markings on its scruffy coat. The other came up to the man's knees with a short red coat and a big round head; both dogs shared their owner's muscular physique.

Lilly's eyes focused on the owner again. "Where did you come from?"

"Sorry, didn't mean to scare you, just out for a jog." He had a faint, intangible accent. "I'm Francis." He held out his hand.

"I wasn't scared, just surprised." Lilly reached over his extended hand for the box, but he pulled back from her.

"I've got it, you get the door."

She hesitated, opened her mouth to renounce his kindness, and then thought better of it. She bent down to snatch up her keys that were sprawled across the pavement.

"Just moving in?"

"Yeah," Lilly yawned lazily.

She opened the door, but before she could hold it open, Francis was already holding it for her.

49

"You are too cheery for a Sunday morning."

"You kidding me? It's the best time to be cheery."

Francis followed her up the steps to the top floor. Fumbling with the key, she tried to think of an easy way to say thanks that would also make him leave her alone to move in, in tranquil silence, as she had pictured.

"Oh! We're across from each other."

She turned to him, trying to wipe the grimace off her face before their eyes met. "Neat."

"When are you bringing everything else? I have a truck--"

"No truck needed. I've only got what's in my car. Thank you though." She took the box from him and set it down inside. Lilly made sure to stand in the doorway to block his view of her empty apartment.

When she turned to shut the door his eyes were set on Lilly's make shift bed. Lilly prayed he wouldn't bring it up; there was a discomfort in someone learning the way she chose to live her life.

"So there's more?"

She nodded and stepped past him down the stairs, determined to enjoy her morning silence. Overly kind people made her uneasy. Kindness often leaves you vulnerable to be stabbed in the back. At least that is what life had taught her. Bad things had impressed many things on her.

"Two's better than one." He followed her down the steps, leaving his dogs unattended at his own apartment door.

Lilly took a deep breath, giving up on her quiet morning.

Francis bounced ahead and held the door open for Lilly. She tried to smile back as a thank you, but watched as her forced smile made him look away uncomfortably.

I suck at being nice, Lilly thought.

The questions were what Lilly feared the most. If she let him in he would start asking where she came from, what life was like back home. Then the worst of it, why and how had she left her family? Lilly felt her hands go clammy as she considered all the questions.

She popped the trunk of her car and grabbed trash bags full of clothes and linens. As she turned from the trunk she braced herself for more conversation, small talk. But he just smiled and grabbed a few things to bring in for her.

With his help it only took them a few trips to get everything unloaded. Lilly was grateful for his help and that he had ceased his conversation making, likely based on Lilly's poor social skills. That was ok though, she was willing to accept that in exchange for silence.

With the last box in her hands she stared out over the lake and surrounding woods. Beyond the lake were a few row homes and single-family homes, but more trees and bushes blocked most of them.

The trunk of the car slammed shut. She turned; Francis had closed the trunk after snatching up the last two bags, and was walking back towards the apartment.

Lilly quickly locked her car and pulled the apartment door open for Francis.

"Thank you."

Walking up the steps Lilly could hear him inhale a good bit and realized what was coming. She braced herself for the questions.

"I have an extra mattress and some other things in my storage unit, if you'd like them. I don't need them anymore."

Lilly looked surprised by his generosity.

"That's very nice of you, but I don't want to be any trouble." She opened her apartment door.

"No trouble at all," he said, and sat the bags down by the others in her living room.

"Really, it's fine. I'll probably go out sometime this week to get furniture." She assured him, but his raised eyebrow showed that he didn't really believe her. Lilly didn't even believe herself.

"I'm Francis, by the way." He held out his hand once again. "Francis Wills."

"You said that already…"

Francis stared, and then added, "And you are…"

"Oh, Lilly Guthrie." They shook hands.

They stood there for a moment in the silence. It wasn't awkward, he was very easy to be around and silence never bugged Lilly unless it bugged the other person.

"Well, I have to go to the store and all..."

"Oh, of course!" He turned to his own apartment, where his dogs still sat, waiting patiently. "This is Cuff and Link." He pointed first to the big dog, then the smaller dog.

"Cute, they're really good dogs."

"They can be. It was nice meeting you, Lilly."

"You too." She smiled back weakly as she closed her door behind her.

———————

Was Dad angry when he got my letter? How was he going to explain why I left to Emma? And my friends... Lilly felt an unbearable pressure weighing down, a realization that maybe they needed her even though she didn't need them anymore. The 'light hits' station droned on in the grocery store, keeping her from screaming.

She wandered through aisle after aisle without placing a single item in the cart.

Over the last six months, Lilly had been so consumed in getting out she had stopped talking to her friends back in Adrian. But the more she secluded herself, the more her friends sought her out. Stacey text or called almost every day. Her voice always sounded so peppy on the phone and Lilly knew if she ever answered with her braced, irritated voice, it would probably ruin her day. Stacey would undoubtedly be distressed over Lilly's absence.

Grabbing a bag of rice, Lilly shook her head.

"No regrets," she muttered.

The real concern was being the new kid that got tormented for showing up in the middle of senior year. Wakefield was populated enough that hopefully she could slip into school under the radar. As long as no one *really* noticed her Tuesday she could get away with not talking to anyone until graduation. Other than Francis, he would be persistent. Lilly smiled thinking of Francis.

"Old Bay..." she picked up a yellow tin filled with spice. She stared at it puzzled for a moment, before putting it back on the shelf.

The food she had selected slid across the belt at the register. It was mostly freezer snacks, cereal, and a few things for lunches. Lilly bit her lip, having no idea if she had chosen the right things. At home her dad always did the grocery shopping. Lilly cooked sometimes, breakfast mostly, because her dad left for work so early, but they ordered out a lot, too.

Lilly's father, Simon, hadn't been grocery shopping in ten years when their mother passed away. He was just as confused as Lilly trying to remember what their family ate on a weekly basis. Eva had been their rock.

The young cashier stealthily slid, nearly threw, the items across the scanner. Her nametag read 'Hello, my name is Kathy, I'm here to help *you*'! Kathy stopped when she got to the apples, sitting them on the scale and then punched in a code. Lilly had never noticed that before.

"Thanks," Kathy said as Lilly bagged the groceries.

"Sure… are you hiring?" Lilly felt her cheeks go red as soon as the words escaped her mouth. Her heart pumped a little faster when the girl looked up at her.

That was a dumb question to ask a cashier.

"Yup." Kathy nodded towards the sign on the front window and continued scanning items.

Lilly could have slapped herself in the forehead, if it wouldn't have drawn more attention to herself. She had consciously observed the sign when walking into the store, "We Are Always Hiring!" She hardly noticed a brick wall in front of her face when the timing was right.

The embarrassing burn lingered on her face longer than she would have hoped. It would have been nice to touch her cold hands to her cheeks or run out the door into the cool air, but she stayed in line trying to look normal. Kathy finished bagging the groceries and rested them in Lilly's cart.

"Eighty-five seventy three," Kathy said pleasantly.

Without looking up, Lilly searched her wallet. She handed Kathy the money and waited for her change.

"There are applications at customer service." Kathy pointed behind her. "You should apply, it'd be nice having you around." She held out Lilly's receipt and change.

"Thanks."

"Can I have an application?" Lilly murmured.

The woman at customer service looked up at her. She was in her late sixties, her short curly hair was mostly gray and her face was starting to fold in on itself. Her nametag read 'Mildred'. As Lilly approached, her expression was a little angry and it seemed to say, 'go ahead, challenge me, complain. You'll be sorry.' But at Lilly's question Mildred's face brightened.

"Oh!" Mildred reached under the counter and revealed an application. "What position are you looking for?" Her eyes were glued to Lilly's face, taking in every move, every expression.

Putting two and two together, Lilly realized no one liked to work here. *Run!* She thought.

"Cashier…?"

"Oh, we really need a cashier! Are you a citizen?" Mildred's eyes narrowed as she stared Lilly down.

"Yes."

"We could have worked it out if not." Mildred grunted as she looked through stacks of papers. "When can you start?"

"Tomorrow..." Lilly replied. It was too late to go back now, besides she needed the money.

"Wonderful! You just fill this out and bring it back tomorrow."

"Wonderful."

Climbing the steps, arms full of groceries, Lilly wondered if Kathy would bug her for information tomorrow. Francis hadn't, yet, but Kathy was her age, and peers always ask questions.

Lilly put her key in the lock then stopped, mid-thought, and did a double take.. Her keys clinked back and forth against the door as Lilly let them go. To the right of the door was a king sized mattress, a dresser, microwave, and a large box with various kitchen and household items.

The mattress looked brand new, to the point she expected to find a tag or plastic wrap on it. The dresser was nothing short of beautiful with a dark cherry finish, roses etched into it all along the edges with a vine and thorns, and legs that turned out underneath it.

At first, Lilly was irritated that her dad or Vincent had already been able to find a way to send furniture and then she realized that there was no way they could have. No, there was only one overly kind person who would have gone to such lengths to get this to Lilly by tonight: *Francis*.

With gritted teeth she let her groceries and purse slip to the floor. It was clear there was no getting rid of him now. By taking the furniture she would always owe him. Lilly was raised better than to refuse it, even if it meant giving up her solitude.

Letting out a good pounding on his door she shouted loud enough for the neighbors to hear, "Francis!"

To her surprise the dogs did not bark. When Francis appeared at the door, Cuff and Link were sitting next to his sofa calm and content, wagging their tails.

"Hey, Lilly." He looked surprised.

Her eyes pierced up at him. She was so intent she missed the smell of fresh cut roses, but none in sight, and the strange carvings in the frame of his door. The carvings were so small the doorframe just appeared dirty unless you looked close enough.

"Yes?" He questioned her expression.

She lost her anger in his kind eyes, her arms dropped from her hips, and she let out a sigh. "Francis..."

"Yes?" His lips curled at the corners, trying not to smile at the challenge of emotions Lilly was clearly working through.

It was evident to Lilly that her feelings were obvious to Francis. She was a book sprawled out for anyone to read. Or help or kick to the curb or take home for their own use.

Her eyes drifted over Francis's sleek muscular body, encompassed by his perfect stature and affable presence. She couldn't yell at him. Even so, she faked an angry voice. "Francis."

Francis took a step back.

"How do you expect me to get all this into my apartment *alone*?" She crossed her arms and harrumphed a little for effect.

What had appeared to be fear slipped from his face and he smiled. "You just can't be happy with what you get, can

59

you?" Francis's shoulder brushed against her as he walked past her towards the mattress in the hall.

"Thanks," she groaned, which of course made Francis laugh. Lilly shoved him with her shoulder in jest.

CHAPTER 6

"When we long for life without difficulty, remind us that oaks grow strong under contrary winds and diamonds are made under pressure."

Peter Marshall

A comfortable mattress and a good night's sleep was easily the best gift Lilly could receive. The entire bedroom consisted of the rose detailed dresser, a few knick-knacks, and the bed, which took up most of the room.

The family room was completely empty except for a few boxes and a TV that was a late add-on from Francis. He insisted that he no longer needed, nor wanted, it but Lilly was skeptical.

She considered that maybe Francis was more lonely than kind. Before he left he offered to go furniture shopping with her, as he claimed to know where to get the best deals on home furnishings. The thought that she had found someone in her mother's vein of shopping scared her.

She had tried her best to push him out, but Vincent was still in her thoughts. Since he left for college, she had only seen him twice. Once was a holiday and on the other occasion he had really needed to talk to Dad. "God knows why," Lilly grumbled, as she dressed for work in her only white button down and black pants.

"Always too busy saving the world to worry about us. Well, I'm busy putting my life back where I want it to be." She straightened her shirt in the bathroom mirror. At least she could look good despite her anxiety towards starting a new job.

"The produce codes are in here. If you have any problems, page me." Mildred slapped a stack of stapled papers on Lilly's register. "Except don't page me, I'll be busy."

The two-minute crash course from Mildred hardly meant anything to someone who had never worked at a grocery store before. Lilly stood panicked. "What about-" Lilly started, but Mildred was already gone.

She smiled uncomfortably at her first customer. Well, itch ointment and energy drinks would have to be her first test.

It was getting into the heat of the day and customers were piling up. Kathy looked pissed; more people were in her line, most likely because they didn't want to be stuck in Lilly's slowpoke line.

"Sorry." Lilly winced, as she couldn't get the register to open. She jiggled the register and tapped buttons, but it wouldn't open. "Oh no." The entire order voided.

"Great!" The customer threw his hands in the air.

Kathy stared up at Lilly like she was ready to scream and shake her.

"Hang on." Kathy nodded to her customer and swiftly slid behind Lilly's register.

"I'm sorry…"

"It's ok, no biggie, see." Kathy smiled and pressed a few buttons. The register opened and Kathy snagged his change while the receipt printed. She handed them to the man. "Thank you for your patience. Have a great day, sir."

"Thanks." He stalked off.

"You're doing great." Kathy reassured Lilly and shuffled back to her own register.

Lilly didn't feel like she was doing great.

Lilly's face contorted at all the produce the next customer had.

She stared down at a strange pear-like fruit. *Sure, a pear*, she guessed and thumbed through her cheat sheet.

"Hey!" Kathy snapped. "It's papaya, 3303. And the limes are 4948." She didn't even look at Lilly as she spoke.

"Thanks," Lilly murmured.

"Ask me for the codes, I'll tell you as you go." Kathy's expression was flat and indifferent, but she let out a simple smile to the customers when needed.

"Travis to the front, Travis to the front." Kathy's voice echoed across the intercom.

Eventually, a crummy looking kid with long greasy hair stumbled to Kathy's register. His hair was dyed black, with long blond roots, and his bad hygiene proved his dislike for his job, or maybe life in general. His shirt was un-tucked, and he wore torn up skate shoes and saggy pants.

"What?" he grumbled.

"Don't *what* me, do your job, bag." She pushed boxes of cereal towards him.

Instead, Travis turned to Lilly.

Kathy glared at the back of his head in a way that could have made him burst into flames. He grabbed the groceries Lilly had scanned and bagged them.

"Kathy wanted your help." Lilly's voice wavered as she scanned more quickly.

"She," Travis glared back at Kathy, "can handle 'erself."

"Just make yourself useful, Travis," Kathy huffed.

Lilly looked up at Kathy for her approval. She just shook her head and continued to work.

"So, uh, name's Travis."

"I noticed." Lilly nodded towards his nametag. "Have a good day, ma'am." She tried to smile at the departing customer, but the woman just sauntered off.

"Ya really have a knack for makin' people happy," he leaned forward to look at her nametag, "Lilly."

"Tell me about it." She held up honey crisp apples. "Hey, Kathy."

"Apples have stickers, Hun. A lot of produce does."

She looked closer at the apples and punched in the code from the sticker.

"So, what's the story Lil?" Just one side of Travis's mouth curled up in a grin at Lilly.

"It's Lilly. And what story?"

"Oh ya know, how'd you end up here? You in college?"

Lilly felt the blood rushing to her cheeks. "Look, I don't know you--"

"Yeah, but where do you go to school?"

Lilly stopped scanning. She counted to three in her head and tried to give him the benefit of the doubt. Travis clearly didn't know when to stop; social cues were not his thing. "Look, Travis, why don't you go find someone else to *help*?"

He glared, and then in an eerie change of emotion smiled a wicked little smile and strolled away.

Kathy and Lilly exchanged an agreeing glance and then got back to work. Most of the day slipped by the same way. Travis came to talk every so often and the customers didn't end. Thankfully, Travis left as things slowed down, or rather, Mildred made him leave.

"Why put up with him? He hardly works," Lilly asked, staring out into the dark parking lot.

"People quit so often. Travis can be helpful, sometimes."

Kathy pulled herself up on the counter behind her register and exhaled; Lilly followed suit.

"The first day's the worst, especially a double. It's easy from here on out."

"Easy?"

Kathy shrugged, cracking open a tin of mints, ate one, and then threw the tin to Lilly. "So, how *did* you end up here?"

Lilly bit her lip and her cheeks swelled with blood. "I needed a job, just moved here."

"Ah. Where from?"

"Adrian, Michigan."

Kathy jumped down to ring up a customer. "You stickin' to the states startin' with M?" Kathy was impeccably serious.

Lilly laughed, and then looked to Kathy to make sure she was actually joking. Kathy raised her eyebrows. "Yeah, something like that." Lilly felt another question coming, so she gave in before the inquisition started. "I start at Wakefield High tomorrow, do you go there?"

Kathy's face lit up. "Yup! What teachers do you have?" She bagged the customer's food while they ran their credit card.

"Don't know yet, I get my schedule tomorrow."

"Have a great day." Kathy handed the customer their receipt. "Wait, what year are you?"

"Senior."

"Oh! Are you taking Health? Sign up for Conway's 4th period Health class! It's so easy! Make sure you don't get Briggs though, he's crazy."

"What does he teach?"

"Trig. Well if you can, get period three gym with Wells. I don't have any friends in gym, it's so boring…"

"I love gym."

Yet another person had seeped their way into her life, but like Francis, Lilly was thankful for Kathy's friendship. She knew she'd be lost at work without her.

CHAPTER 7

"...A bear rushed out of the bushes and made straight for them. One of the men, quick as a flash, took to a tree... The other, seeing he had no time to escape, threw himself flat upon the ground, pretending to be dead."

Aesop, The Travelers and The Bear

"See you tomorrow, find me in the morning!" Kathy waved as she got into her car.

As Kathy drove off, Lilly began stressing over tomorrow. Then a slow sharp pain rose from the palm of her hand, up through her wrist, distracting her thoughts.

Footsteps sounded behind her.

Her feet scurried faster, not wanting to turn and see her assailant. The pace behind her quickened as well. There was a slight clanking of keys or change in a pocket that was meant to be muffled. Change in a pocket meant a man. The pain in her wrists flared up again and she couldn't help bounding to an all-out run, her face went pale, and her heart raced like a drum roll.

Just a few paces from her car, she fumbled with her keys, her fingers shaking and stiffening, and turning all in their own way, distracted by the pain. It was as if each finger thought their way was the most important one and couldn't find common ground to work together. Lilly winced as her keys clattered to the ground. The footsteps pounded closer and she dared not look.

"Lilly," panted the owner of the footsteps, Travis.

A hand crept over her shoulder as she bent down to get her keys. This was it, wrists blazing and a strange kid grabbing her, that moment she had considered buying a taser for. Though she knew she would have tased herself if she had one and just made things easier for her stalker in the end.

"I wanted to talk to you." Travis's hand clutched her shoulder and pulled her up. The way his eyebrows crept around his eyes and he grabbed her, she feared what he was capable of.

"I really need to get going, Travis."

His grip was so tight she wanted to cry. The pain in her wrist rose higher as she tried to pull away. "Look, don't go, I-"

"Travis, please, leave me alone."

He pulled her towards him so she was only inches from his greasy hair that swayed in front of his face. His eyes were terrifying, picking up the florescent lights in just the wrong way. "Why don't you like me Lilly? You don't even know me."

"Because I, you, you're--"

"Travis, knock it off!"

They both twisted to find a kid, about their age, but tall as the sky and skinny like a child that played too much to think about food. He was attractive just the same and would be even more so once he filled out.

"This doesn't concern you, Quinn," Travis sneered.

"You'll be making better friends with Thaddeus if you don't leave." Quinn drew his cell phone from his pocket and dialed.

Travis looked from Lilly then back to Quinn. He loosened his grip, but didn't desert his position entirely. "How about--"

Before he had a chance to finish his sentence Quinn took Travis by the shirt, causing him to let go of Lilly. He tried to fight, but Quinn easily pushed him away. Travis landed a few feet off, knocking into a light post.

Cussing, Travis paced into the shadows between the shopping center buildings, but not without glancing back once more at Lilly.

Frozen, Lilly stared blankly at the spot Travis had landed, trying to decipher what had just happened. Like so many others, Lilly wondered, what did Travis want with her? She turned to Quinn who watched as Travis disappeared into the darkness. When he caught her gaze stepped towards her with his hand outstretched. Lilly took a step back.

Quinn stopped. "Sorry, I didn't mean to scare you. I, I work over at the bowling alley." He pointed to the bowling alley catty-corner to the grocery store. "I was closing for the night and I saw Travis, and you..."

Just wanting to go home and prevent another bad scene, Lilly nodded and backed up to her car door.

"Travis can be a real jerk, but don't judge us all by him." Quinn turned towards his own car.

She was still in shock from what had just happened. Quinn had put himself on the line for her when he didn't know her from Adam, but Lilly was scared to take that same chance.

"Thanks," she mustered.

Quinn smiled. "Any time, my lady!" He bowed, and his lanky, long body nearly touched the ground.

Lilly's heart fluttered and she tried not to laugh, but it slipped out anyway. That was promising enough to Quinn to shoot her a wink before getting into his car.

He waited after getting into his car, making sure Lilly got safely into hers, before driving away.

As Lilly drove away, Zeke stepped into the light between the grocery store and the bowling alley, Gahd just a few steps behind him. She placed her decrepit hands on his shoulders. He tensed and grimaced, but he didn't move.

72.

"And?" She whispered in his ear, so close he felt her hot breath sizzle.

"When faced with danger she won't fight back, not even when being influenced. She just freezes up."

Gahd snorted and took a step back, in deep thought.

"Why wouldn't she fight back, Gahd? What does it mean?" Zeke stepped closer to her.

"Generations..."

"Who is she?"

Gahd grinned up at the sky. "She doesn't even know what she is. Won't even fight back... time to open the gates tomorrow, Zeke. Open the loathsome gates," she cackled as she Faded.

By the time Lilly reached her bed, it was just before midnight. Francis and his all too calm dogs had stopped her on their way out for a late night walk.

"How's the new job, kid?"

"Fine," she grumbled sleepily.

Francis stood patiently with Cuff and Link.

Lilly reminded herself that she had a nice comfy bed thanks to Francis. "I made a friend, she goes to Wakefield High."

"That's great."

"Yea," she felt cheerier, "Kathy works with me, she gave me some pointers on teachers for my schedule." Lilly was surprised by her own openness and continued to share, as Francis was really listening to her every word.

In the midst of their conversation a petite Russian woman entered the building and Francis stopped her. "Oh, Sonya, this is Lilly. She's new to the building. Lilly this is Sonya."

"Nice to meet you." Lilly awkwardly waved.

"My daughter Lyda and I live in 'A'." Sonya pointed downstairs. "If you ever need anything, don't hesitate."

"Lilly is across from me." Francis continued a conversation with the pair of them.

He must have given Lilly Sonya's life story in about ten minutes, when the two women could think of nothing but sleep. Sonya politely excused herself after glancing at her watch.

After Sonya left, Francis wished Lilly a good night.

At this point, Lilly was curious if Francis ever slept or worked or if he simply waited in his apartment for a chance to talk with someone. Was it possible someone so young didn't work or was he older? Or maybe he was sitting on a fortune.

Lilly curled up in bed, dropping her thoughts to the comfort of sleep. She had checked that the front door was locked and her apartment was empty, twice, before she had gotten into bed.

CHAPTER 8

"Good art is not what it looks like, but what it does to us."
Roy Adzak

Lilly's sleep was a jumble of half hours and staring at the clock, wondering how God-awful her sleepless face would look in the morning. The bad dreams when she did sleep didn't help.

In her dreams back home she was always running from something. She never knew what she ran from, but she would run as fast as she could, like a hamster on its wheel, going nowhere. The fear she would get caught by whatever was behind her always woke her up, only to fall back asleep and dream it again.

But tonight she kept falling. The dreams started pleasantly, strolling through the park, but then she would try to jump across something. Unable to make the jump, it turned into a free fall with no end in sight. Over and over she experienced the same dream. Each time it ended with her falling into bed, sweat dripping from her forehead.

By the time she had given up on sleep it was six in the morning with plenty of time to waste before the late bell. She organized her clothes in the dresser, ate cereal, packed a lunch, and finally stared around her shell of a home. With nothing else to do, she left for school early, figuring maybe the guidance counselor would let her get a head start on making her schedule and she could get a good look around school.

But when she pulled up the student lot was nearly full. Students loafed around in their cars, some with music blaring, others looked like they had spent the night, with blankets, sleepy eyes and all. Some kids were already chatting near the school with their morning coffee and doing homework or goofing off.

Lilly pulled up next to a Volkswagen Bug that two girls sat awkwardly on the hood of. Both girls stared Lilly down as she pulled into the spot. They wore skinny jeans and one had long blond hair while the other had short curly black hair. Before she was even able to get her things together and rush off to the office, one of the girls was at her window.

"Excuse me," her knuckles tapped against Lilly's window, snapping like a hungry alligator's jaws.

Lilly turned to find her curly black hair all in her face and her lips shaking, perturbed with anticipation. Lilly considered simply going home and starting school tomorrow. This day could end now, before she had to listen to what this girl had to say. Or maybe ignore her, step out of the car and walk away from her without a word. The thought was all too tempting.

Lilly closed her eyes. "One, two, three…" she breathed.

"Hello, Earth to Donna Day Dream!" Her dangerous knuckles rapped on the window again.

Lilly threw the car door open, almost hitting the girl. "Yeah?"

"Finally! You can't just park anywhere you want, you know. I was saving this spot for Jen, she *always* parks next to me."

"Oh." Lilly licked her lips, trying to find that tone in her voice that sounded like she cared. "Maybe this Jen girl should get to school a little earlier if she *has* to park next to," Lilly paused to look her up and down, "you every day. Anyway, I'm already parked."

Lilly grabbed her backpack and threw it over her shoulder. A simple thought made her smile: *at least she isn't super happy I parked next to her so we can be BFFs forever and swap boy stories!*

"Alright, I get it, you've got issues with parking, I'll help you back out." She stepped to the back of the car and positioned herself to direct Lilly safely out of the spot.

"No, it's not that." Lilly shut her car door and crossed her arms. "I'm just, parked."

Lilly got too much satisfaction in destroying the girl's morning. The fact that her day seemed to revolve around that one parking spot made Lilly even less likely to care. She felt like a mother weaning her kid off a pacifier.

"Get over it."

"Ok, look," the girl ground her teeth back and forth, her fists clenched. "What's your name?"

"Lilly."

The girl bit her lip, her face twisting, trying to figure out what to say. "Look Lilly, we park here every day, and I don't want to, but if I have to, I know every guy in this school and--"

"Oh come on Erica, I know everybody in this school *and* their mothers, what's that got to do with a parking spot? Which, might I add, was made for exactly that, parking." Zeke slipped in between Lilly and Erica.

Lilly recognized him as the same guy that stood outside the school in the rain on Saturday. He wore a leather jacket today too, except this jacket had two stripes across the front, not like the old fashioned one he had on the other day.

Zeke leaned back against Lilly's car and took Erica's hand in his hand. "Now tell me Erica, what would you say to all those people you know? When it seems--Lilly?" He turned to Lilly, who confirmed with a nod. "Lilly here, obviously has no idea about your arrangement with Jen. It wouldn't be fair to just slander her name." He let go of her hand and it fell back at her side.

"Ok, Zeke..." Erica's voice was defeated.

Screeching on its breaks, a jeep pulled up behind Lilly's car. The driver stared at Lilly, then Erica. "But you have to deal with Jen." Erica dashed back to sit on her car.

"Starting the morning out right," Zeke muttered sarcastically, slapping the hood of Lilly's car.

Their eyes met for a moment, but Lilly dropped her gaze.

Zeke strolled up to the Jeep, whose driver was undoubtedly Jen, judging by the glare aimed at Lilly.

Lilly took the opportunity to gather the rest of her things and lock her car before anyone else tried to get her to move for some incredibly childish reason. Her car door squeaked and shut a little too hard, as she looked up and found Zeke at her side again.

"That's it, you're just gonna leave? No thanks?"

"So, not only are you intrusive, but you're so impressed with yourself that you need me to be just as impressed with you?" Lilly blurted out, each word begging herself to stop in her head.

"Wow," he grinned, "you're sassy."

"Look, I just want to get to class."

"Class? The class that starts in twenty minutes?"

"Yeah... I guess so." Lilly's eyes fell away from him. He tended to stare her right in the eyes.

"I'll let you in on a little secret Lilly, I know it's your first day and all, but--"

"How do you know that?"

Casually, he shrugged and put his hands in his pockets.

"Like I said, I know everybody. But I don't know you, which means you're new. Anyway, you should know, nobody goes to class this early, in fact, it might be best if you're late."

The thought crossed her mind to give him her best confused puppy-dog face and then wander off, but decided against it.

"So let me get this straight, it's uncool to go to class early, but it's completely normal, and possibly even cool, to get to school a half hour early."

"Exactly. Most of us just like to make sure we get the right parking spot." He winked.

"Oh, is that it? Where's your parking spot?"

"You see that black Trans Am?" He pointed to his left where a group of kids in khakis and collared shirts were.

Lilly nodded. He must be one of those rich kids whose parents bought them everything.

"That's my car. My spot."

Staring into Zeke's eyes, Lilly began smiling and listening intently to him. His eyes were a deep dark blue and his hair just barely draped over the top of his eyes.

Zeke went on about the specs of his car as Lilly simply continued to stare into his eyes. He placed his hand on Lilly's shoulder and immediately Lilly's gaze dropped down to her burning wrists. Zeke's touch was poison to her wrists.

"Let's go for a ride," Zeke coaxed, "we'll be back by second period."

Blood rushed to Lilly's cheeks and her body stood paralyzed as her wrists burned.

Their conversation had drawn in quite a few ears. Everyone seemed to be staring, or pretending not to.

Lilly craned her neck up to look at Zeke. His lips curled into his cheeks as he wisped his hair away from his face. "I'm Zeke North, by the way. Let me introduce you to some people before we go."

As he spoke his hand drifted from shoulder, to arm, trying to direct her towards his car.

Overcoming her paralysis and throbbing wrists, Lilly whipped her arm away from him. "No."

"Come on," Zeke said surprised. Clearly no one had ever told him no before. He grabbed for her arm once more, but Lilly pushed him away, making him fall backwards a few steps. He narrowly missed hitting the pavement.

"What's your problem?"

Staring down at her hands, Lilly realized that she didn't even understand her own actions. This strange pain she had gotten since childhood always signified that something bad was going to happen. Zeke seemed genuine; he had helped her and been kind like Kathy and Francis. And yet...

Zeke stepped towards her again.

"Back off."

He stood stunned.

"Hey, Lilly!" Kathy broke the silence that covered the student lot. She wrapped her arms around Lilly. "Morning, Zeke." She waved, breaking away from hugging Lilly. Kathy turned herself and Lilly towards the school. "Come on, I'll show you where the office is. Maybe they'll let me help with your schedule, that way we'll definitely have classes together!"

Staring a hole into the back of her head, Zeke stood in place, cracking his knuckles. Taking a peek back at Zeke, Lilly cringed. He actually looked angry with himself as he bit his lip, pivoted around, and ambled back towards his car.

Zeke punched in a text on his phone, 'UNABLE TO INFLUENCE TO SKIP. GIRL APPEARED PANICKED.' He slid his phone into his pocket.

"Hey, Jen!" Kathy yelled across the parking lot.

Jen waved at Kathy and glanced over Lilly grumpily.

"You know her?" Lilly's eyes grew wide.

"Of course I know her, I waved."

"I don't think she likes me."

Kathy raised her eyebrows.

"I sorta took her parking spot... and refused to move."

"Refused to move? Really Lilly, that's how you make friends your first day? You really hit it off with Zeke, too."

"It's too early."

Lilly felt her cheeks burn. Knowing how obviously uncomfortable she must have looked only made things worse. Kathy glared at Lilly and then to Lilly's surprise, Kathy laughed.

"Jen always gets ticked off about parking. If she parks under the trees she ends up with leaves and bird poop on her seats. But she's too lazy to get her butt out of bed early enough to get the spot she wants. To add to it, she won't put the top on her car until it snows. Don't worry about her, she's in a constant self-inflicted bad mood."

Lilly's cheeks were still hot, but she too laughed.

"Kill 'em with kindness." Kathy winked.

CHAPTER 9

"All that we see or seem is but a dream within a dream."

Edgar Allan Poe

Strutting past the rest of the line students in the office, Kathy stepped right in front to the secretary. They spoke for a moment then the secretary glanced at Lilly. "You'll have to wait here until the announcements have commenced. Then Ms. Lyons will see you." That was all she said before turning to another student.

"Sorry," Kathy muttered, "I wanted to stay, but she said I can't. Just try to get C lunch with me!"

Before Lilly had a chance to say anything back, Kathy was down the hall talking with someone else. With her tour guide gone Lilly was struck with worry. Everyone had a place to be, something to do; all Lilly had was anxiety.

She sunk down into a chair and leaned forward to stare at her feet for something to do. Letting herself peek every so often, Lilly noticed all the cliques. The secretaries behind the counter gabbed about their weekend over coffee and the geeky kids waiting to do the announcements were chatting up a storm.

Then there was Lilly, always out of place. She sat back in her chair and stared up at the ceiling. What had made her so sure that this would work? Some silly note that could have meant anything and been from anyone? The thought crossed her mind that she hated school and had ultimately been trying to escape it, but school was school anywhere.

Lilly inhaled. *This is for Mom, I will find out who led me to Wakefield and what Mom's life was like here.*

One of the secretaries cleared her throat. Sitting up, Lilly noticed everyone was standing and had their hands on their hearts for the Pledge of Allegiance. She stood reluctantly.

As soon as it ended she sat down and listened as the reminders of football practice and algebra help after school droned on. By the time Lilly was contemplating taking a nap, a plump middle-aged woman with flowered glasses appeared in front of Lilly.

"Lilith Guthrie? I'm Ms. Lyons." She sounded like she was chewing gum, but she wasn't. It was likely a side effect of trying to talk through such large cheeks.

"Lilly."

"Lilly, then." She led Lilly to her office.

The seats were fake brown leather, so old the cracks showed the itchy yellow stuffing inside. There were boxes of folders and papers piled all around the room and filing cabinets lined the walls. A photo of a very rotund bullmastiff sat on her desk.

"Let's see," she sat down behind her desk and opened a manila folder newly labeled, 'Guthrie, Lilith'. "Ms. Guthrie, eighteen. According to your file you've been taking British Literature, Health, Trigonometry, which it seems you *failed* last year... well this won't work," she bit the end of her glasses as she spoke making it even harder to hear her. Placing her glasses on the desk she looked down at Lilly condescendingly. Her eyes gleamed and her stare made Lilly lean back awkwardly. "You'll have to take gym again. We encourage physical activity here."

"Ok," Lilly said slowly so she didn't burst out laughing at the irony.

Ms. Lyons twisted her glasses around in her mouth. Lilly cringed at the thought of all the germs she was picking up.

"You had planned on doing work study; only being in school half the day. That won't be possible, as you will need another phys ed, history, and a science credit. The requirements in Maryland are a little different from those in Michigan. You may as well take a few more classes to round out your schedule, it will look good for college applications." Ms. Lyons put her glasses back on, looking smug.

88

"Wait, no, I need to work, I need the money, I--" Lilly jumped to her feet, panicked as to how she would afford everything if she was in class all day.

Before leaving Adrian she had planned everything, everything except for different credits in Wakefield. She would have nowhere to live if she didn't demand work-study. Lilly found herself leaning over Ms. Lyons' desk ready to lay into her.

Ms. Lyons sat grinning, listening to Lilly's defiant outburst. Slowly Lilly sat down. She wouldn't mention the need for money or protest again, it perked too much interest with Ms. Lyons.

"I'm sorry Lilly, there's nothing I can do. To graduate from this school you'll need Chemistry, Phys Ed, and one history elective. Many seniors enjoy World History, lots of war." She thrust her hand like Rosie the Riveter and smiled at the word war.

To keep from cursing, Lilly bit her lip and nodded. She would find another away to make enough money, working nights if she had to.

"World History it is then." Ms. Lyons tapped at the keyboard, clearly delighted to be crushing dreams today.

The typing stopped and the printer buzzed to life. "Your first class is Latin Three. It's right down the hall in room 215.

She handed Lilly her schedule. Lilly stared down realizing she forgot to ask for Kathy's recommendations.

1. Latin – Healy
2. Chemistry – Jones
3. Trigonometry – Briggs
4. Health – Conway
5. British Literature – Pearce
    "C" Lunch
6. World History – Olson
7. Gym – Robinson

At least one class she shared with Kathy and lunch, but she also had Briggs, who Kathy had warned her about. Math wasn't Lilly's best subject, nor her worst, but either way she didn't want a difficult teacher. She opened her mouth to ask Ms. Lyons to change it, but Ms. Lyons spoke before Lilly had a chance.

"One more thing before you go. I noticed that you've moved here on your own, but with permission from your father?" Her unrealistically sweet tone rang, the one Lilly had heard from every therapist or person trying to get a tiny bit of emotion from her growing up.

90

"I--"

"Why don't we talk about it? Were things ok at home?"

Lilly felt her face go red and her stomach churned. Her cheeks burned so hot with anger that her mouth wouldn't move.

"Did you move here because of your mother?"

Her heart was beating so fast that Lilly was sure Ms. Lyons could hear it.

"Let's talk about your mom."

"It's none of your business." Lilly lost sight of her lockjaw.

Ms. Lyons leaned forward, her eyes narrowed, and something terrible was about to seep from her lips when--

"Cynthia, we need to talk about that smoke corner." The door flung open and a broad shouldered man in a police uniform hulked over Lilly. "Oh, sorry, you're busy."

"We're finished." Lilly threw her backpack over her shoulder and rushed for the door.

"Oh, no we are *not!*" Ms. Lyons stood.

The officer took a step in front of the door to block Lilly. "Should I go?"

"No, Thaddeus, wait right there."

To Ms. Lyons' dismay, Thaddeus shrugged and stepped out of Lilly's way. Lilly turned and stood behind Thaddeus, using him as a buffer.

"Don't worry, I'll be sure to stop by if I'm in the mood to discuss *my* business."

Ms. Lyons's eyes were blazing. No doubt she wanted to yell, but she couldn't make a scene in front of Thaddeus. Before Lilly dashed out the door she looked up at Officer Thaddeus, who winked down at her with a widespread grin.

CHAPTER 10

"Two things cannot be in one place. Where you tend a rose, my lad, a thistle cannot grow."

Frances Hodgson Burnett

Hardly anyone noticed when Lilly showed up late to Latin. They were reciting verb endings when she handed her schedule to Mrs. Healy. She took a seat in the back of the class, finally gaining some invisibility.

There was an entire wing of the school that she couldn't find after Latin, almost making her late to Chemistry. Thankfully she ran into Thaddeus, who directed her. Mrs. Jones welcomed her to the class, giving her a seat and a book. It all made for a cozy second period until Travis walked in ten minutes late. At first he walked right past her, but it was inevitable.

"Whoa, Lil!" He sat next to Lilly, flinging his hair back.

"Leave me alone, Travis."

"Travis Alexander, that is *not* your seat." Mrs. Jones diffused the situation in seconds.

Travis looked up at Mrs. Jones to argue, but she just pointed at his actual seat.

After sitting through Chemistry with Travis staring at her, Lilly didn't think anything could be worse. Yet somehow

93

Briggs was worse--Kathy's warning held true. His classroom was insufferably hot, but according to Kathy, who had to suffer through the class with her, he never let anyone open the windows. He always wore long sleeved shirts and rolled them up. Apparently he liked to sweat, a lot.

"Someone should introduce short sleeved button downs to him," Lilly whispered to Kathy and she giggled loud enough that Briggs turned around.

"What? Question? Anyone?" He looked helplessly around the room with his sweat darkening the pits of his shirt. After looking around like a paranoid owl through his glasses, he turned back to expose the sweat stain down his back.

Kathy and Lilly looked at each other and laughed quietly.

"The key is layers." Kathy took off her cardigan.

Besides the heat, Briggs was hard to follow; he just threw the equations up on the board all class. When asked a question he would answer with solving an equation on the board, but no real explanation. Most students had given up on asking questions.

"What class do you have next?" Kathy snagged Lilly's schedule as they pushed through the crowded halls.

"Health."

"Me too. Oh, we have lunch together! I guess they were nice about your schedule."

"Ms. Lyons basically just handed it to me, then harassed me about…"

"About any little smudge she could find on your record?"

"Yes! What's her problem? If it wasn't for the, uh, the officer, I would have been stuck there with her a lot longer."

"Thaddeus?"

"Yeah!" They walked into Health class.

"Thaddeus loves to bug Ms. Lyons. Somehow, he always shows up when she's making someone's life miserable."

"Good, she deserves it." Lilly bumped into a dreamy, sky-high muscular guy with a varsity football jacket on, knocking her books onto the floor.

"Sorry, hun. Here you are." He bent over and picked them up for her, and then winked as he handed them back.

Lilly watched him sit down next to a girl with beautiful shiny blonde hair down to her waist. Lilly stared at her until Kathy grabbed her shoulder. "What, what?" Lilly asked.

"That's Derek, and his girlfriend Elaine. He's a total man whore and she's over protective."

"Sounds like the perfect couple."

95

"Not the best couple to get in between," Kathy said.

For the majority of class, Elaine threw Lilly impenetrable glares. The class itself was bad enough, and worse yet Lilly had suffered through the same unit earlier this year in Adrian--the reproductive systems. With every other word from Mr. Conway there was a giggle from the girls or an 'oh yea' from the guys.

By the time class was over, Lilly was thoroughly reminded of why she hated school.

Kathy and Lilly parted ways; after Lilly received much needed directions to British Literature, where they discussed a chapter of the novel they had read the night before. This left Lilly with nothing to do, as she had never even heard of the book.

Lunch, then two more classes and her first day was over, Lilly reassured herself as she stepped into the overcrowded lunchroom. She didn't even think she could find an empty seat let alone next to anyone she knew, but Kathy quickly waved her down.

As she got closer to the table, Lilly was surprised and considering standing if she had to. It wasn't just Kathy, Jennifer and Erica were there too. She was ready to turn around, but Kathy got to Lilly first.

"I, uh…"

"Don't worry, we all had a good laugh about it already." Kathy jumped up and dragged Lilly over to the empty seat next to her.

"There's always room for one more headstrong girl at our table," Erica laughed, but Jennifer showed no sign of forgiving Lilly. "Right, Jen?"

Jen rolled her eyes and promptly got into the lunch line.

"Jen'll get over it," Kathy said.

"Eventually," Erica said.

"Hopefully not too soon, this whole deathly stare thing is amusing," Lilly replied.

They all laughed.

"Jen just has a tough exterior, inside…"

Quinn sat himself at the end of the table and leaned his guitar against the wall. The girl who sat with Erica on the car and two guys Lilly hadn't met sat with him. The girl didn't even bother making eye contact with Lilly.

"I'm Amir." One of the guys waved, he spoke with a Middle Eastern accent and was tall and skinny like Quinn.

"Hey." Lilly waved.

The other kid wasn't nearly as tall as Quinn or Amir, but broad in the shoulders with thick curly hair.

"Ah, who's the new chick?" The guy nudged Quinn.

"Lilly." Quinn nodded.

"And you are?"

"Andy, football team--"

"Local hot shot."

"He's Jen's boyfriend," Kathy added, probably afraid Lilly would say something rude about Jennifer.

"Andy."

Lilly shook his outstretched hand.

"This is Dawn, she sits with us when she's not skipping." Kathy pointed to the blond girl who had sat with Erica on the car before school.

"Psh," Dawn uttered.

"Alright, who's up for some tunes?" Quinn pulled his guitar from its case.

"No, no more Green Day!" Kathy said.

"Or 'Stairway To Heaven'" Dawn chimed in.

"Ok, ok, calm down, I'll play something different today." Quinn sat on top of the table and started strumming a light tune.

Jen sat back down next to Andy, who put his arm around her and much to her annoyance, stole her food.

Lilly's attention drifted over to Zeke and a short blonde haired kid. They were hunched over by the windows at a table with Elaine and Derek, looking at something together. Then, they both stepped back and Zeke handed the blonde kid something very small. He put it in his pocket and Zeke walked away, towards Lilly. Zeke ambled past Lilly, his eyes fixed on hers.

"Lilly." Kathy nudged her.

"Hmm? What?"

"Come on, the bell rang."

Everyone else at the table had already scattered.

"Oh."

"Why were you staring at Zeke? You think he's cute?" Kathy raised her eyebrows up and down a few times.

"Cute? I don't know about cute... I, uh, I don't want to make bad with any other friends of yours, but Zeke's kind of strange, don't you think?"

"Well, yea, I guess he does kind of live in the past."

"No, like, this morning, he grabbed me."

"Grabbed you? I always thought he was nice."

Lilly stared at her, confused by her sudden mystical tone.

"If you just go out those doors and to the left, you'll see the trailers for your next class." Kathy pointed, completely oblivious to Lilly's stare.

CHAPTER 11

"Integrity is doing the right thing, even when no one is watching."

C.S. Lewis

Following Kathy's directions, Lilly turned left and just around the corner were the trailers, which is exactly where Officer Thaddeus and Ms. Lyons stood guard. Thaddeus had a female student by the shirt and snatched a pack of cigarettes from the girl's pocket. It was unorthodox to see a kid held by her shirt these days, but Thaddeus didn't seem to care what society thought.

"Hey, Lilly." Zeke came up from behind her and blew smoke in her face.

"Thaddeus is right there," Lilly coughed and waved the smoke away.

Since he did seem to know everyone, Lilly was willing to play his game and get on his good side.

"Thanks, doll." He winked and smiled his sickly sweet smile that made most girls blush. Zeke put his smoke out and hurried up ahead to the blonde kid from lunch.

"Hey, John..." Zeke whispered to him.

Then, all at once, a few things happened that made Lilly's first day one of the worst she had ever had. Thaddeus

100

let go of the girl as if he caught a scent. Then whatever Zeke had handed John at lunch fell from his pocket.

Without thinking, Lilly ran towards Zeke and John.

"Hey, you dropped something!" she shouted as she stood by the tiny plastic bag.

John looked back at her like she was crazy, standing there paralyzed.

"Who dropped this?" Thaddeus bent down and picked up the small bag. He looked to Lilly waiting for her answer.

John still stood there, but everyone else had walked away or taken just a few steps away to separate themselves from him.

Suddenly, her wrists burned. She closed her eyes, and then opened them again. Lilly's eyes met John's and that was all the recognition Thaddeus needed. Within seconds Thaddeus was hauling him off to the office.

"What's your problem?" John sneered.

"Shut up." Thaddeus pushed the kid forward and gave Lilly a reassuring smile.

Everyone stared at Lilly. And Zeke, the one who had given John the drugs in the first place was nowhere to be seen. Somehow he had dodged Thaddeus's attention and slipped away without anyone noticing.

Lilly plowed through the crowd, ignoring their stares and whispers. She ran up the steps to Trailer 1, flipped open the door, and found Zeke sitting in the back of the room

"Great. You're in my class."

She took an empty seat across the room from him, only for Zeke to move next to her.

"You probably just got John expelled, you know."

"Awesome, thanks for that bit of news." She turned away from him, but he knew how to make himself seen. "Very convenient you weren't there."

"Is that why you left your other school? You couldn't stop pissing people off?"

"No, I left because--" Lilly stopped.

They stared uncomfortably.

"Leave me alone, Zeke." Lilly changed seats.

When bell rang and the rest of the kids in the class strolled in from the commotion outside. Students pointed and whispered about John, Thaddeus, and *Lilly the nark*.

For Lilly the room was spinning, life itself was spinning. In three days she had managed to move across the country, get a job, make two good friends, and create a name for herself at Wakefield High. The only problem was that that name was '*nark*'.

She tried to stay under the radar in the next two classes, but somehow everyone knew her face now and there was a story behind it. "That's the girl who told Thaddeus" or "She's the one who got John expelled," they whispered. Even Jen looked pleased as Lilly walked by her on her way to gym.

They were out of uniforms, so Lilly had to sit on the bleachers while everyone else played basketball. Not only did she have to retake a class she had already taken after making half the school hate her, she had to sit out of the fun and watch as the ditzy girls missed the backboard all together.

"Lilly!" Quinn called as he bounded up the bleachers in one of the grossly thick red and black gym uniforms.

Lilly smiled at the sight of him.

"You're not playing?"

"I mean, I would, but, they're out of uniforms. Apparently I need one to participate," Lilly sighed.

"Sorry…" He placed his hand on her knee and her heart jumped three feet from her chest.

"Quinn, get your ass down here," shouted Zeke. He and Amir stood at the bottom of the bleachers.

There was a flash of orange and Quinn's hand shot in the direction of Zeke's voice, just barely catching the basketball hurtling towards his face. "Why, you ready to lose *again*, Zeke?" Quinn winked at Lilly and hurdled down the bleachers.

Lilly had wanted to trust Quinn after last night, but he was a friend of Zeke's. Lilly shook her head. "I don't need friends," she muttered.

Quinn and Zeke played one on one at the opposite end of the court from the girls while Amir waited for his turn. Quinn was red faced, while Zeke barely broke a sweat. They hit shot after shot back and forth, until Derek appeared. Zeke exchanged a few words with Derek and Derek's eyes met Lilly's for a split second before turning his back to her.

Water splashed against Lilly's cheek, distracting her. Looking up she found a tiny hole in the ceiling leaking above her. She moved over a few feet on the bleachers. When she looked back Zeke was gone. She scanned the entire gymnasium, but no Zeke. Quinn was shooting HORSE with Amir now.

Lilly stared back up at the crack in the ceiling and watched as the water dripped down. She wondered how Emma's day was going.

"Miss Guthrie, Lilith Guthrie." Mr. Robinson waved from the bottom of the bleachers.

Lilly jumped. The gym was now empty except a few students setting up for the basketball team. "Oh, I prefer Lilly, Mr. Robinson."

"Ah, Lilly, you've been dismissed. You'll have a uniform tomorrow, I promise. Hope the first day wasn't too bad." He smiled, and then turned to help the students set up.

CHAPTER 12

"These two she would have liked to keep for ever just as the way they were, demons of wickedness, angels of delight, never to see them grow up into long-legged monsters."
Virginia Woolf, To the Lighthouse

Zeke sat on the ledge of the school roof. He closed his eyes as he repeated the words in his head. If he didn't get them exactly right, he might not release the right demon. He himself might get eaten, or worse. Once more he repeated the words in his head, then opened his eyes. Carefully, he drew a knife from the sheath at his side and took to his feet.

Standing on his toes on the ledge, Zeke raised his hand as high as he could. "Arbitra invoco ex inferno desumant aliquem daemonium pompæ multitudo." Zeke thrashed the knife all the way down to the surface of the roof. It left a large hole in the human plane, cutting the sky like a curtain revealing the darkness and fire of Hell behind it.

A talon clutched the side of the curtain, pulling it back to reveal more of Hell. Zeke flinched slightly, but he stood his ground as a beak snapped shut inches from his face. Zeke bowed to the shadow of the demonic creature that revealed itself from the hole he cut in the universe. It was so vast it had to bend over to step out of the hole.

The locker room was empty; students were making their way to their cars, on school buses, or walking home by now. Lilly had had the foresight to bring a lock for her gym locker; leaving her backpack in it with the hope she could participate in her regular clothes.

Lilly sighed as she removed the lock and hauled her backpack over her shoulder. "Day one, done." She rested her head in her hands. "Could have been worse."

"How much worse ya thinkin'?"

Lilly jumped two feet, as Elaine and two other girls emerged before her.

"That was real messed up whatcha did today." Elaine tilted her head, signaling to the girls. They surrounded her.

"Look, I didn't mean to, I just--"

"You just got the best wide receiver this school has ever seen expelled."

"What did John ever do to you?"

Elaine threw the first punch, knocking Lilly square in the jaw. She didn't have time to react before the next punch came flying in. In a matter of seconds she was on the floor curled up, trying to protect her head and gut. They didn't hold back, kicking from all sides. Blood dripped from her face in more than one place and her shin throbbed like it had been split open.

But after a few kicks, Lilly caught the girls slowing down and forming a pattern, taking turns kicking her. Lilly had never been in a fight before and the shock was wearing off. Quickly she put a few things together; her backpack strap was still wrapped around her right arm and had all her text books in it that she had received in each class today and there was the back door to the locker room.

In one smooth motion, as smooth as she could after being beaten up, Lilly jumped to her feet, extended her right arm with her backpack in it and spun once in a circle. She caught them by surprise and nailed all three of them in the gut with her hefty backpack, knocking the wind out of them. Without missing a beat Lilly, leapt over the locker room bench and ran for the back door.

"Get her!" Elaine wiped blood from her lip.

With the others only a few feet behind her, Lilly pushed off the balls of her feet with every bit of strength she had left, trying to ignore the pain in her shin and ribs. She flung the back door to the girl's locker room open. The doors were locked from the outside, but unlocked from the inside. She threw the door shut and put all her weight against it, bracing herself with her feet.

The girls ran into the door, pushing it open a few inches. Lilly's heart raced. She only had a few moments left to run, secure the door, or get her ass kicked again.

"Shoot..." Lilly rested the side of her head on the door and shut her eyes, trying to think what to do.

"I'm gonna kill you!" Elaine shouted through the door.

Lilly took an empty binder from her backpack and with a bit of elbow grease folded it in half. Elaine threw her weight into the door, cursing, pushing the door open almost a foot. They took a few steps back ready to do it again. Using the brief lapse to wedge the folded binder between the two looped door handles, Lilly secured the door.

She took a step back and watched as they hit the door again, but the door didn't budge. They banged on the door and hollered, but the binder didn't break.

"The power of physics," Lilly grinned.

She leaned back, letting the door support her. It was hard to believe something so small could hold back so much force.

But her triumph was interrupted when something dripped onto the grin stretched across her face. She wiped it with the back of her hand. It wasn't blood. Again something dripped near her eye. There was a quick sharp click, click sound, and slapping of a tongue against... something that was not lips.

Slowly, Lilly craned her neck. Above her perched a bird, or maybe a man, or a dragon? Lilly's heart threw itself repeatedly against her chest begging her to run. The creature clutched its two feet over the edge of the roof. Each foot had three scaly finger-like appendages with talons at the ends and something that must have been like a thumb off to the side. Its rear end curved into a large pointed tail that twitched over its back. It was hunched over, with two stocky arms and hands much like its feet.

The skull was that of a man, but it turned from side to side like a lizard. A large beak poked out where the mouth and lips should have been, if it had in fact been a man. Its eyes were so dark they hid amid the creature's dark color, but the piercing glare froze Lilly with fear.

Her mind begged her legs to run. She couldn't take staring into the thing's eyes any longer. Still facing it, she slid backward a few feet and slipped her backpack on over her shoulders. With each step away she took, the creature's leathery wings rose inch by inch until she was twenty feet away and it carried a fifteen-foot wingspan. That's when they began flapping. Without wasting another second, Lilly broke her eyes away from the beast and threw her legs into high gear.

The school was a series of wings that stuck out from the main hall. She sprinted out of the alcove to the end of the wing. The creature was rising up off the roof as it flapped its wings. At the end of the wing was a steep grassy hill and a gravel path leading to the student parking lot. Knowing the hill would slow her down too much, Lilly threw her body sideways and squatted down like a snowboarder, sliding across the gravel. Her hand grazed the gravel as she rolled to a stop.

The creature was jetting directly at her. It opened its mouth and emitted a horrible screech. Click, click, screech. Click, click, screech. Its forked tongue spit out.

"Lilly!"

She looked up ahead and Francis stood at the corner near the student parking lot, calling to her. His dogs flanked him, snarling and snapping, as if wolves ready to fight a larger predator for a meal. In his hand Francis had a long whip with a golden fall at the end.

"RUN!" He shouted.

Lilly ran towards him at full force. The creature close behind her, Francis raised the whip in the air just as Lilly reached him. She slowed.

"Don't stop running."

Lilly turned the corner and kept going until she found Francis's truck. It was the only vehicle left in the parking lot except hers. She glanced at her car considering just leaving, but she decided to wait by Francis's truck.

Francis flipped the whip into the air. The creature had lost track of Lilly, focusing in on Francis and the dogs now. It threw its wings straight and still into the air, halting it in place. It tread the air, snapping back at the dogs.

"Back to Hell!" Francis roared.

He flicked the whip at the creature. The whip wrapped around its neck and the golden fall snapped against its face. Francis jerked the whip back. The creature screamed so loud Lilly threw her hands over her ears in the parking lot. Then the creature turned bright fiery red and crumbled to a pile of dust.

The dogs ran to the dust, snarling and barking in circles around it.

At the other end of the school Zeke puffed on a cigarette, passing an icy stare to Francis.

The dogs looked up from the pile of nothing, their lips raised and growling at Zeke.

"C'mon dogs." Francis turned towards the parking lot.

"What was that, Francis? What's happening?" Lilly's horrified voice echoed as soon as he turned the corner.

"Get in the car." He threw the whip in the back.

"Tell me what's going on."

"Do you trust me?"

He opened the passenger door.

"Yes."

"Then please get in the car, before more come." He took a deep breath and gave Lilly a reassuring smile. Following his gesture, Lilly jumped in the car and he closed the door behind her.

"DOGS!" He shouted as he got in the driver's seat.

Cuff and Link came hurtling around the corner barking and leapt into the bed of the truck just as it sped off.

CHAPTER 13

"I laid the manuscript down, consoled to find that my father had had a peep into that mysterious world, and that he knew Mr. Raven."

George MacDonald, Lilith

It had been nearly ten years since Francis had last seen Lilly. There had been a few close run-ins with her before she moved to Wakefield, but the promise to her mother had been no contact. The best way to keep her safe was to keep her off the grid. Francis himself was far from off the grid, so, grudgingly, he left Lilly and her family alone.

Speeding down the road, Francis went over all of Eva's last wishes in his head. Francis snapped out of his daze and realized he had brought them to the park, Oregon Ridge. Not home to the apartments or somewhere one might consider safe like a police station or hospital to tend Lilly's wounds. He pulled the truck into a spot closest to the park entrance.

Lilly threw the truck door open and trudged out into the woods. Even limping she moved pretty fast. She had tried a few times to ask Francis what all this was, how he knew she was in danger or how he had gotten rid of that *thing*, but Francis didn't even look at her the whole ride. In the silence, her fear turned into a fury.

114

Taking to the woods, she considered where she would move since it was clear Wakefield was not safe.

Link licked Francis's ear through the small back window of the truck, breaking Francis's trance. Lilly was disappearing into the woods when he pulled the keys from the ignition and went running after her.

The dogs traveled behind him, getting distracted by smells and sounds here and there.

"Lilly, wait."

Looking over her shoulder Lilly sneered at him.

"Let me explain. I should have told you sooner, but I..."

Francis stopped. Lilly continued, but slower now.

"I was hoping I wouldn't have to yet..."

"Tell me what? That I should skip town? That I moved to the twilight zone? Just leave me alone Francis, I'll wake up soon, or I'll move far from this hell." She could feel the tears welling up in her eyes as this terrible day came crashing down.

"At least let me take you home."

"I don't even know you, you don't owe me anything."

"You do know me, Lilly."

Lilly ignored his words, "I'm leaving Wakefield in the morning."

"You can't run from this. They'll follow you wherever you go. Your mother, Eva, tried that too. It does no good."

Lilly stopped at his words.

"And what do you know about my mom?"

Lilly turned and stepped towards him with determination.

They were pretty deep into the woods by now. It was growing dark as the old trees were bushy and hid the sun even in the less dense areas.

"This," Francis pointed around them, "is where I met her. She ran here the day she saw her first demon and I was sent here to tell her what her father couldn't. Your grandfather that is; he had passed before Eva reached high school. I told her, just as I am here to tell you, what your mother can't."

His eyes met hers and Lilly felt herself slink to the ground of the forest.

"Demon? But, that's not possible…"

Lilly thought back to the creature flying towards her. She shuddered. It was hideous, terrifying, and had to be a dream.

"What other explanation is there?"

Francis knelt down at her side.

"Government science project gone wrong?"

Francis shook his head.

"Aliens? Drugs?"

"No, Lilly."

I'm dreaming, she thought and buried her head in her hands.

Does this feel like a dream? Francis pinched her leg.

"OW!" She leapt to her feet. "What's your problem?"

Demons live among us. Angels too.

"Well fine, I'll believe a demon. I saw it, but angels? Not a chance in--" she stood still. "Your lips, they're not moving."

Because you're hearing my thoughts.

She stared, unable to make wrong or right, up or down of the situation. Then she burst out laughing. "I've lost it, I have officially lost my mind. Well, it was bound to happen one day."

She threw her hands in the air, succumbing to a resting spot against a tree.

Francis knelt again and placed his hands on her shoulders. Within seconds her breathing evened and her mind quited. *No, you can hear my thoughts because I'm an angel. Or I was, I mean--*

"Let me start over."

Lilly waited.

117

"You and a select few of your ancestors, including your mother, are special protectors of your realm, here on Earth. You are here to keep balance between what is right and wrong, good and evil. You and you alone are the Keeper of a deadly sword, known as the Ferryman. You must learn to wield the Ferryman and protect your world from destruction."

She stood uneasily, staring at the ground then up at the sky. "Mom used to ramble... when she was sick, that demons were trying to kill her."

"We're not supposed to talk about it." He shook his head. "But, she was very sick in the end."

Lilly's eyes drew sharp and she wished he wouldn't talk about her.

She was my friend. Francis's voice was in her head again.

"You're lying."

"How do you think you ended up here? *I* gave you the idea and the means, the money."

"The note..."

"Let me show you." Francis stepped towards her and reached his hand out so he was just close enough to touch her.

Lilly nodded slightly.

Francis placed his palm on the side of her head and his thumb just touching her forehead and closed his eyes.

Abruptly, Lilly's eyes shut and her body jolted. Her mind filled with memories she had forgotten and images she never knew. First was the time she got lost in the mall, but this time she saw the man's face that saved her. It was Francis. All those years ago, Francis had been the one to shield her from that strange man. *Thank you*, she knew he heard her.

The next memory, Lilly sat on the day bed in her little sister Emma's room. Emma was in the crib and Vincent stared out the window irritably. It was night and Eva was screaming, screaming about the demons. Her dad popped his head in, "Thank you, Francis," Simon said.

Lilly looked over and Francis sat next to her on the day bed. "I'll stay as long as you need me, Simon." Francis's smile was weak and worried. He looked exactly the same then as he did today.

Other memories and images came flooding in, more than Lilly could handle. She saw Francis in her room, putting the yearbook, box, and money under the floorboard.

That memory faded and Lilly saw her mom with a sword as tall as her waist, its hilt was silver and black with a straight guard and a circular symbol on the pommel. The blade itself was glowing blue, with four or five runes on it. Eva struck a ten-foot, black-skinned demon with horns the size of her forearms with the huge sword.

Lilly jumped away from Francis, out of breath.

Francis lowered his hand.

"No pressure, huh?"

Francis shrugged, "Just telling it how it is."

"Dad knows why I'm here, then?"

"No. He and Vincent's memories were wiped as well. For their protection of course," he added when Lilly glared.

"Aren't angels and demons here to keep the balance between good and evil?"

"Yes and no; there are rules. I'll teach you." He put out his hand for her.

Instead, Lilly stepped right up to Francis's face, her neck craned up to meet his eyes. "And what if I chose not to accept this... duty?"

"You could. I would want the money back." He chuckled, but Lilly stared angrily. "Demons know who you are now, they would find you like they did today."

"Why? I don't know anything!"

"They want the Ferryman and they'll torture you to find it. They can't ever find it or possess it, Lilly. It would mean the end of our world. Decimation."

"But I don't have it, I didn't even know about it until a few minutes ago."

"They don't know that, they just know that you're the Keeper."

"Aren't they listening now, wouldn't they have followed us?" Lilly looked around the woods suspiciously.

"There are rules in this world for angels and demons. For the most part they can't just show up here, they have to be let in. I'll teach you, as I did your mother."

"How do I know you're not a demon deceiving me?"

"What does your gut tell you? Do you get a bad feeling from me?"

Lilly looked him up and down, slowly taking in his calm demeanor and concerned eyes. "I get bad feelings a lot, pains in my wrists. But you make me calm, peaceful, even when I'm angry."

Because I'm an angel.

"This is strange enough without your thoughts in my head." Lilly snapped.

"Sorry."

"It's ok. I mean it's not. But..."

They stood awkwardly, not knowing where to go next.

"So where is my sword then?" Lilly grinned. There were bound to be some perks to this and a cool sword was one.

"It's hidden. When your mom got sick she hid it because she couldn't keep it safe anymore. She should have left you clues to where it is. And only you would know or be able to get it from that place."

"No Francis, this is the first time I've heard of it."

"She wouldn't have been able to come right out and say it, you were too young."

"Oh!" She pulled the locket out from under her shirt. "This locket she left to me, it has a key in it."

"Yes."

"But I don't know to what."

"It will come to you when the time is right." He brushed his hand across her back. "Until then I will teach you. About demons, angels, defending yourself…"

"If I agree, then you have to tell me about my mom." Lilly put her hand out for him to shake.

"It's a deal."

They shook on it.

The wind brushed from tree to tree, rustling dead leaves as if they were giving a sigh of relief, the leaves gliding down and finding their resting place.

Without discussing it, the pair walked towards the parking lot.

"How did you know I was in trouble?"

"It's an angel thing."

"You don't look like an angel. Where are your wings?"

122

"I... I'll explain everything later. How about we get you cleaned up?"

The fear the demon had cast over her made her forget all about getting beat up. She embraced the pain. Now that the shock was gone she limped on her left leg, where blood had bled through her pants. Touching her cheek, she winced. She breathed and made the realization her ribs more than ached. It was possible one or more were broken.

"I need a hospital, Francis."

"I know."

CHAPTER 14

"The antidote for fifty enemies is one friend."

Aristotle

"Francis, the hospital." Lilly said as he parked his truck outside their apartment building.

"I have better medicine than any hospital."

Lilly was nothing if not confused, but decided not to argue as stranger things had happened in the course of the day.

Francis pointed out the markings on his doorframe, he told her how the Latin, runes, and some angel magic made a force field. It could protect against weaker demons and evildoers, though not all.

"You can stay here. It's safer than your place, at least until I get a chance to bind your apartment as well."

"If staying here means no demons, I'm a go," Lilly laughed.

While she cleaned up in the bathroom, Francis threw a quick meal on the stove, then sprawled his *healing agents*, as he called them, out on the coffee table.

"Sit." Francis nodded to the couch when she exited the bathroom. He sat on the coffee table and squished a glowing bright green goop onto his hand from a toothpaste tube.

Lilly sat across from him. "How is toothpaste--" before she could continue, he was smearing it on her face. "Oh gross! Ow! Francis!" Lilly pushed him away.

Francis waited, letting his hands rest on his knees palms up, watching as Lilly's face contorted under the gross feeling of the goop. In a matter of seconds the cuts on her face disappeared and the color faded from the deep bruising to a light red. The moisture in the gooey substance seeped into her skin, soothing it, leaving a crusty glue-like substance behind.

"That... Wow." Lilly touched the layer over her skin. "It feels so much better." She sounded grateful, but tired.

"You should trust me more. Go wash your face, then apply it twice more and you should be back to normal. Do around your ribs and shin, too."

Continuing in the bathroom, Lilly watched her skin heal before her eyes. The second layer went deeper, soothing her muscles. The third her bones no longer ached, they even felt stronger than before.

"I understand, I will... Yes, I promise, Francis..." A female voice rang as Lilly exited the bathroom. Francis stood blocking the door.

Francis turned as he heard Lilly creeping down the hall. "Thank you, Sonya." He shut the door.

Lilly leaned to see, but with no luck. "What was that?"

"Just Sonya." Francis shrugged. "Dinner?" He motioned to the small dining room. There were two plates on the table. Grilled chicken, a bowl of diced browned potatoes, salad with fruits and vegetables, and brown rice were laid out on the table.

Lilly's heart jumped. She couldn't remember the last time she had actually sat down to dinner with someone. Back home her father may or may not have been working or she refused to leave her room. Dinner involved conversation, questions, sharing, feelings...

Francis sensed her panic and exhaled. He sat down and made his plate without a word, but his eyes were set with worry.

Lilly thought first of running back to her apartment or just straight for her car, but her feet were cemented to the carpet and her car was still at school.

She closed her eyes and counted down from ten in her head. *Ten, it's just dinner. Nine, what happens when you lose your temper? Eight, he made you dinner and you're hungry. Seven, you'll lose your temper and yell at him for no reason. Six, he's shown more care for you in two days than your family has in years. Five, end it now before he has a chance to let you down. Four, if you leave now you'll never learn about your mother. That's why you came here, isn't it? Three, is learning about your mother worth letting someone down? Two, your mom would want you to get to know him. One, your mom wouldn't want you to get hurt, she'd want you safe, never feel the pain of loss again. Zero. Absurd. You're being absurd, it's just dinner.*

When she opened her eyes Francis was eating, ignoring her.

She sat down and made a plate.

They ate in silence. After a few minutes Lilly's shoulders loosened. There were no questions, no sharing of the day's events as recapping would be destructive at this point. When they finished Francis took their plates to clean them and Lilly cleared the table. While she put things away Francis took a pillow and blanket from the closet and sat them on the sofa.

"You can have the bed." He pointed down the hall.

"No."

Not wanting to argue, Francis simply turned, then clicked to the dogs who sat beside the sofa. They didn't budge. "C'mon, time for bed." He waved them towards the bedroom, but still nothing. "Have it your way." His voice was cross with them and then softly, "Good night, Lilly."

"Night," was all she could muster as he retired to the bedroom. It had been years since she gave anyone the courtesy of a goodnight, unless forced by Emma.

After his door clicked shut, she rested her head on the fluffy pillow. It was clearly brand new and had to be patted down a few times to be comfortable.

Cuff circled three times, scratched at the carpet, circled once more, then laid down against the sofa right at her head. Link jumped up on the sofa and followed suit, but laid against Lilly's feet. With the dogs sleeping, Lilly breathed in deep and exhaled, hoping it would release the tension. It did not. Of all the things that had happened through the course of the day she had three things left on her mind.

If Francis was an angel, and she had met a demon today, what did that make Zeke?

The memories Francis had given her back. She couldn't help replaying them over and over again.

And lastly, why was eating dinner with Francis more difficult than anything else today? There was an aching feeling of how poorly she treated him, despite his kindness. She exhaled, hoping admitting it would help her, but it did not. She lay awake for what felt like hours fighting her conscience.

In the next room Francis spoke to what any human would think was an empty corner, just air. But Francis was not human. He could see the enormous male angel standing before him, whose head nearly touched the ceiling, with shaggy black curly hair. His slacks and shirt were both black and tight on him. Two light jackets draped loosely over his shirt.

There was no expression on the angel's face, his features were well defined, his posture nothing less than perfect. He held a tall white staff with a blue orb at the top in his left hand. The tips of his white wings could be seen near his bare feet and the tops bowed around his shoulders.

Francis hunched over on the corner of his bed. His eyes were glassy and blood shot. He rubbed his clammy palms.

"Who let her get like this?"

The angel said nothing.

"She's damaged." Francis threw a fist at the mattress, which did nothing, barely even made a sound. "What can *I* do to help her now? Years of living disconnected from us, Michael! Look at her! I told you we should have taken her when Eva died." His voice was low as to not wake Lilly, but it spilled with anger. "She would be ready for this if we had."

Michael moved not a muscle nor gave any reaction to Francis's erratic behavior.

"Who forgives all your iniquities; who heals all your diseases. All things are possible." Not even a smile of encouragement seeped from Michael before he spread his wings and vanished with one wisp of his wings.

"Of all beings you are the one who could help her." Francis snapped. "Why you refuse to speak with her…"

Francis calmed and rested his hands on his knees. He was glad the dogs were with Lilly and that he had a moment alone with Michael, reminding himself how few his words used to be when he was an angel and how important each word really was.

He lowered his head.

CHAPTER 15

"Logic is like the sword—those who appeal to it shall perish by it."

Samuel Butler

"Did they blame her?" Gahd's voice ebbed through the phone.

"Yes," Zeke replied. He was sprawled across the sofa in his living room, staring at the ceiling. Skoal stared at him from across the room, watching his every expression.

"And have you talked with her?"

"No, not yet, but-"

"But you'll do it tomorrow? Is that the best you can give me? This has to be done on time, Zeke! Did I hire the wrong Half Life?"

Zeke laughed. "You did the *hiring* sweetie, not me."

She growled.

"I'll do what the contract says, when it says it, Gahd."

"And the demon?"

"Francis killed it, like you predicted."

"Hmmm."

"You figure that one out." He clicked off the phone.

"Don't push her buttons. You better hope she doesn't show up here." Skoal warned.

"I hope she does."

"She'd better not. Or were you looking forward to seeing what I can do with my new tongue-twisting manipulation?" Skoal waved his arm, but Zeke started to flip over the back of the couch, and then Faded. He reappeared next to Skoal.

"Play your games with Jaymie. She's not as quick--" Zeke started, but with a flick of Skoal's wrist, Zeke was on the floor.

"You were saying?" He stood over Zeke, grinning.

"At least I can disappear fully." Zeke Faded again, but this time out of sight.

"Yes, well, it takes *living* flesh a little more time to completely master that sort of manipulation." Skoal plopped down in the kitchen, hunched over an old book.

"Look here." Skoal called to Zeke after a few minutes.

Zeke Faded into the seat next to him.

"If the lore is true, not only is the Ferryman real, but there is only one person, from a long line of people, who can possess it."

"Person, as in human?"

Skoal nodded.

"A human is supposed to wield the Ferryman? The sword that kills all, in the hands of a human?" Zeke laughed. He leaned back, now uninterested. "Myth it is."

"No look, right here." Skoal pointed to the strange symbols on the old brown pages. "A human is to wield the Ferryman, as a fail-safe to keep the peace between angel and demon."

Zeke leaned over him and stared at the pages.

"The human world belongs to the humans."

"And the sword is to protect their world," Zeke uttered.

They both looked up from the pages and stared at each other.

"Lilly is the Keeper of the Ferryman," Skoal stated.

CHAPTER 16

"The greatest remedy for anger is delay."

Lucius Annaeus Seneca

When Lilly woke in the morning, both dogs lay across her. The larger one's head rested on her chest and she immediately wondered how she breathed through the night. As she sat up, the front door creaked open and Francis ambled in. Both dogs jolted up, whining and tripping over each other to get to Francis. He knelt down and rubbed their necks, "That's my boys, yeaaa." He grinned ear to ear in the face of his dogs.

"What time is it?"

"Nine." Francis sat a few bags on the table.

"I'm late for school!" She leapt off the couch. She looked down at her shin, surprised that there was no pain after the beating her classmates had given her the day before.

Francis pointed to the dining room table. "Sit."

Her mouth hung agape ready to protest, but she ate it down. Every ounce of her swore rebellion. She wanted nothing more than to smash the chair and saunter off to school. But the question rose in her how school was rebellion and learning about a deadly sword and demons was conformity. The best compromise was to sloppily plop down in the chair and throw her arms across her chest.

"I picked up your car."

"Thanks."

"After school we start training. I teach a self-defense class in the high school gymnasium with Thad at 2:30. I think your friend Kathy usually comes."

"I have work after school."

"Not anymore."

"I have bills, Francis. I-"

"Again, not anymore."

"I can do it on my own, I don't need help!" She snapped as she stood up and pushed her chair out with more force than necessary.

"I know you can. Now you don't have to, Rosie the Riveter."

"I guess I should be thanking you." She grumbled.

Francis shrugged. "Sonya asked if you would take her daughter, Lyda, to school."

"Fine." Lilly turned to leave, then stopped. "Tell me something, something about my mom."

A small smile rose in Francis's cheeks. "Eva... She loved you three more than anything. I never met someone so kind, yet deadly with a sword."

Lilly leaned forward, waiting at each word, wanting more. Her neck craned and she found herself smiling.

"She had a beautiful smile. I think you have her smile, though it's hard to tell. You do it so rarely."

Her lips flattened and her eyes narrowed, staring him down.

Francis laughed, "Go find Lyda."

"So, how long have you known Francis?" Lilly's car engine fired on and Lyda clicked her seat belt across her.

Lyda crinkled her nose and swished her lips back and forth thinking. "Since we lived here, a few years I guess." She nodded to herself, confirming the details. "Yeah, a few years." She locked eyes with Lilly. "He's cool, he always helps me and Mom when we ask. Mom brings him berries from my cousin's farm. He loves berries and watching the sun rise," Lyda stated.

"That's good to know." Lilly chuckled at Lyda's way of telling about Francis.

"Why'd you move here?"

One, two, three… Lilly breathed as blood rushed her cheeks. "I needed a change, I guess."

CHAPTER 17

"What you see and what you hear depends a great deal on where you are standing. It also depends on what sort of person you are."

C.S. Lewis, The Magician's Nephew

Jen was slightly more pleasant this morning since Lilly didn't take 'her' parking spot. School, then self-defense, then schoolwork. It would be a long day, but not nearly as rough as yesterday, Lilly hoped as she strolled the halls with her head down, avoiding the looks from other students. They stared and backed out of the way of the nark; the jocks glared. Kathy acted like nothing had happened. Maybe she didn't even know.

There was nothing to learn in health class except that Lilly was clearly to blame for John's expulsion. Derek ran straight into the back of Lilly's chair in an attempt to knock her out of her seat. But she didn't fall; she kept her feet firm on the floor and steadied herself with her desk. Both Derek and Elaine glowered at her every chance they got, though Elaine seemed more confused, likely by Lilly's *lack* of injuries.

Kathy was something of a safe guard for her; she had this look of death that turned any stare away in a matter of seconds.

Lilly sat silent in the lunchroom as her friends teased each other and shared stories about their day so far. Quinn wanted to see the new horror movie over the weekend, causing all the girls to groan in unison. Lilly couldn't imagine a movie being worse than her real life. She pictured the snapping winged creature hovering above her. Its tongue slapped against its beak and talons raised as it prepared to fly. She jumped from her seat, her eyes wide and heart ready to jolt from her chest.

"The creature was real..." Lilly murmured.

Jen burst out laughing.

"Day two at a new school and girl done lost it." Erica joined in Jen's cackling.

Quinn's fingertips touched Lilly's arm lightly. "It's just a movie. Maybe we could see the comedy with the penguins instead?"

"Maybe," Kathy shrugged, and then turned her back to Quinn. "Who's coming to self-defense after school?"

Lilly forced a smile to Quinn, "Thanks."

As she looked away, she saw Zeke. Her eyes drifted from each different group Zeke visited. He had some weight around here--hipsters, jocks, honors society, the popular kids, anime club--in every group, he knew everyone. As he made his rounds, his hand always fell on the shoulder or maybe a wrist of one kid from each group.

At the honors society table, he put his hand on the shoulder of a red headed girl. She was casually eating her lunch and when he touched her, she didn't even look up at him, she just stood up and walked over to the jock table. A girl that Zeke had already tapped on the shoulder was waiting for her. The redhead handed the jock girl what looked like a lab worksheet. It happened so quickly and smoothly, as if it was planned. Like the drug deal Lilly had already witnessed, except this wasn't drugs and Zeke wasn't dealing. Zeke was just... *touching*.

The girls were back at their tables now, mulling about in their typical lunchroom behavior. Lilly's eyes wandered the cafeteria as she thought of the memories Francis had given her back the night before.

Then, just like that, Zeke disappeared, nowhere to be found in a matter of seconds.

"Lilly," Kathy waved until it broke Lilly's trance.

"Oh, hey." Lilly looked up.

"Friday, you hangin' out with us?"

"Oh Friday? I don't know..." Lilly searched for Zeke again.

"Come on! You don't want to be at home on a Friday."

"So you in?" Erica asked.

"I… umm… What are we doing?"

"Probably go to Hill's Grill again." Jen confirmed Lilly's fear; Jen would in fact be there. "We can't agree on a movie."

"And then avoid going home the rest of the night," Kathy sighed. Everyone nodded in agreement. Going home on a Friday night was not an option.

"Yeah, I'll be there." Lilly said.

"Me too," Amir butted in.

"Girls only!" Kathy threw a crumpled up paper lunch bag at him. Amir blocked it and stuck out his tongue.

Everything went back to normal. Jen and Andy made out, now that no one could complain not to while they were eating. Dawn played a doodle game on her tablet while Quinn, Erica, and Amir argued about how many games the Orioles would win next season. Lilly leaned in to check out Dawn's game when suddenly her wrist pulsed with pain. She gripped it and winced.

"You ok?" Kathy whispered, so she wouldn't bring any more attention to Lilly's grimace.

Lilly nodded. Standing up again, she looked around and found Zeke had returned, standing two tables away. He exchanged words with a boy that barely looked old enough to be a freshman.

"You got a thing for Zeke?" Erica nudged.

"Huh?"

"You keep watching him."

"Oh, no, he just... It's weird how he hangs out with everyone, don't you think?"

"Well, he is like, the most popular kid in school." Jen rolled her eyes.

The bell rang and everyone quickly dispersed. Lilly couldn't help but wonder if they didn't want to be seen with her.

Passing through the halls, the twinge in her wrists started again. "Lilly," Zeke bounced in front of her, grinning. "Might I walk you to class?" He bowed and held his hand out to her.

Lilly pushed past him.

"I can keep you out of trouble." He winked, catching up.

"You are the trouble."

"Ok, ok, I'll take the hit. Yesterday wasn't a good day for you, but it wasn't my fault either."

Lilly gave Zeke a sharp look and she considered decking him, but decided against it as it would only draw more attention to the *nark*. Lilly sighed as they stepped outside towards the trailers.

They stepped in sync with each other. "So is that a yes?"

"We're walking, aren't we?"

"You looked disappointed to miss out on gym yesterday," Zeke asked after a moment's silence.

"I love basketball! Hopefully I'll have a uniform today."

"You any good?"

"I mean, yeah, basketball, softball, hockey, I'm good at most sports." Lilly saw his eyes brighten. "What about you?"

"Basketball is great, but soccer…"

By the time Mr. Olson started class, they had moved on to talking about places they'd traveled. Zeke was naming the states he had been to, though it would have been easier to ask him the ones he hadn't been to. Lilly was surprised by how easy it was to talk to him.

"Who knows the cause of World War II?" Mr. Olson scraped chalk across the board. Lilly had already taken the unit in Adrian and hated it.

"Now, Montana--" Zeke whispered to Lilly.

"Very interesting, Zeke. However, this is not geography. How about you Ms. Guthrie, what caused World War II?"

Lilly racked her brain... *this should be the easiest question.* "Trigger happy barbaric men that would rather kill each other than talk things over," she blurted out.

Her classmates chuckled and egged her on, but Zeke looked annoyed and turned away from her.

"Quiet!" Mr. Olson clapped. "Interesting assessment Lilly, but not what I was looking for. Does anyone have a more accurate response?"

"Trick question, there wasn't just one cause," Zeke said.

"Right you are." Mr. Olson slapped the chalk against the board and made three bullet points.

CHAPTER 18

"Peace cannot be kept by force; it can only be achieved by understanding."

Albert Einstein

Lilly waited on the bleachers for self-defense class, watching Elaine and her crew. They were entirely confused about Lilly's bruise-free face. Lilly smiled, knowing exactly how her wounds healed so quickly.

"Hey, you're here!" Kathy beamed when she walked in the gym. Seeing Kathy, Elaine gave up on the idea of having a moment alone to bust Lilly up again and stopped glaring.

"Yeah, Francis is my neighbor, he recommended I come."

"Any girl in the school would recommend it." Kathy motioned to the line of girls, and a few guys streaming in. Jen was among them.

Lilly looked down at her tattered knock-off clothes, noting the nice name brand workout clothes the other girls wore. The girls with old shorts could pull them off with their skinny or toned legs. But Lilly had neither. No tone, no brand name, and despite her height, she never thought of herself as skinny.

"Come on ladies, quit standin' around! Grab some mats!" Francis strode in with Thaddeus. They chatted while

144

the girls dragged large padded wrestling mats to the center of the gym.

It was strange seeing Thaddeus without his uniform. He wore sweats and a shirt that read *'I can't stop, I won't stop'*. It made him look younger and in better shape than the frumpy uniform made him appear.

Francis took off his tracksuit jacket, revealing his toned shoulders. One girl Lilly didn't know stared at Francis. Distracted, she dropped her mat on another girl's foot and quickly got an elbow to the gut, starting a scuffle.

"Hey! Save it for the class." Thaddeus blew a whistle.

It took a few more minutes to settle everyone down. Francis started the session with a few stretches and had everyone do two laps around the gym. Then Thaddeus worked everyone through simple ways to get away from being grabbed.

"Today you will learn to escape a choke." Thaddeus turned so his back was to Francis. "Francis is the attacker..."

They ran through scenarios where the attacker was in front and behind, showing a few ways to get out of each hold. In one demonstration, Thaddeus even flipped Francis over his shoulder onto the mat. The girls giggled.

"Alright, let's get started," Thaddeus said and helped Francis up. "Who wants to do a demo with Francis?"

Every hand in the class shot in the air except Lilly's.

"Lilly, come demonstrate." Francis waved her over.

He was relaxed and confident, but Lilly panicked. She refused to move except for shaking her head as she glared at him. The other girls looked on, envious that Francis even knew her by name.

"I will." The daydreaming girl who dropped the mat stepped towards the front.

"No." Francis crossed his arms and stared at Lilly.

No way Francis. Lilly thought.

You have no choice, Lozen. Fracnis' voice rang in hear head.

"Lilly," Kathy motioned for her to go.

But Lilly shook her head.

"You're such a wimp," Kathy laughed.

Lilly looked down at her concrete blocks for feet. Kathy pushed her forward. Lilly was leaned back on her heels, but Kathy pushed hard enough to get her on the balls of her feet, trampling to the front of the room. She stumbled up next to Francis and Thaddeus, and tried to keep her eyes on them rather than looking out at her peers.

"Ok, now who knows what to do when an attacker chokes you from behind?" A few hands shot up in the air. "Good."

Lilly dared to take a peek at the twenty or thirty girls watching. They were all intent on Francis, not even looking at her. She exhaled and turned to Francis, a little more confident.

"Face away." He motioned for her to turn around.

When she turned completely away Francis placed one arm around her neck and the other draped over her shoulder.

"So what do you do?" Francis called across the gym.

"Kick him in the balls!"

Thaddeus, who had been quietly at Francis's side, marched out into the sea of teenage girls.

"Oh c'mon…" the girl protested as Thaddeus led her to sit on the bleachers.

"So, what do you do?" Francis asked Lilly.

Lilly wiggled her neck and shoulders, testing his grip. "Hit your side?"

"Good."

Zeke appeared at the edge of the gym, leaning against the wall to watch. Most of the class didn't notice besides Thaddeus, who took a step towards him, but Francis shook his head, stopping Thaddeus.

"The three main points here are feet, groin, and core. After you break free from your attacker you can flip them, or go for the forearms, face, throat, etc." He tapped Lilly's right

147

shoulder. "Then use that as time to get away while they're winded. Go ahead, Lilly."

"Don't hold back," he whispered in her ear.

For a moment Lilly wondered what he meant. How hard she should hit him? Then she considered his miracle goo and decided it didn't matter if he actually got hurt. His body tensed up as soon as she made her decision.

First, she slammed her heel down on his right foot, and then she elbowed him under the ribs. *Not the groin* he uttered in a pained voice in her head. Lilly couldn't help grinning, but only faked hitting him in the groin. As his grip loosened on her neck, Lilly took his arm and clumsily threw him sideways over her shoulder. She felt him push his weight to help her.

At each blow, the class gasped and then stood silent at the clamor of Francis hitting the mat. Lilly shot Elaine a threatening look, but Elaine already look alarmed.

Thaddeus was the first to burst out laughing. The girls around the room lowered their hands from their mouths and looked at each other. "Good job Lil." Thaddeus patted her back.

With that the class clapped and giggled. Francis refused a hand from Thaddeus and helped himself up. Thaddeus gave Francis a friendly punch in the shoulder, continuing to laugh, but Francis kept a stark expression.

"Good." Francis placed his hand on Lilly's shoulder and pointed her back towards Kathy.

"Break out into groups of three: attacker, civilian, and spotter. Let's use a little less gusto than Lilly though, ok ladies?" Thaddeus called, causing the class snigger.

"Thad and I will be coming around to check on your form."

Lilly paired with Jen and Kathy, working through a few different self-defense exercises and even some boxing. Thaddeus and Francis stopped students every so often to show them what they could do better or to show the class the next exercise. After forty-five or so minutes everyone was sweating and smiling at their new, confident moves.

"Alright ladies, see you next week! 'Til then, stay safe," Thaddeus called, as the chatter got louder and the work died down.

Everyone pulled their mats back to their resting places and left after high fiving Thaddeus and Francis. Elaine was one of the first to leave, but not without throwing Lilly a nasty look.

"Good job today Kathy, Jen. You both showed a lot of improvement." Francis smiled.

"Thanks!" Jen beamed.

"We've been practicing."

149

"Good." He turned to Lilly. "Can you stay after for a minute?"

"Sure," Lilly replied, knowing *her* self-defense class had yet to end.

"I'll be right back." Francis walked towards Zeke.

"Ooooo, stay after?" Kathy giggled after Francis was out of earshot.

Jen made smooching noises.

"Ew, gross, he's my neighbor." Lilly wrinkled her nose, but couldn't help her eyes wandering to Francis, who took the opportunity to turn and wink at her, which didn't help her case.

"Oh, right," Kathy said sarcastically with a smile.

"Seriously! How old is he even?" Lilly retorted.

Jen shrugged. "Who cares?"

"Have fun." Kathy winked. She and Jen made faces and giggled their way out of the gym.

Lilly just shook her head and found a place on the bleachers to wait for Francis. The muscles in her arms and thighs hurt. The fifteen-minute boxing session with ducks, kicks, and punches woke up all her dormant muscles. Over the past few years she hadn't done much in terms of organized exercise. As she massaged her forearms, she watched Thaddeus pack up his belongings. He noticed her and smiled.

"How do you like Wakefield so far?"

"I'm not really sure yet."

"Francis tells me you're his protégé." His eyes lit up green.

Lilly jumped from the bleachers, "What? What are you?"

His deep husky laugh made his chest shake. "You'll find most of us here in Wakefield are a little *different*." He left without answering her.

Lilly shook her head in amazement.

Francis's conversation with Zeke must have gotten heated because neither of them looked happy. Francis turned his back on Zeke, who looked crazed. Zeke gave him a little shove, but Francis just continued toward Lilly without faltering. A cruel, arrogant smile crept over Zeke's face and he disappeared before her eyes.

"Francis!"

He shook his head. "Sooner you learn, the better." He motioned for her to follow him to the mats that had been left out.

"How'd he do that? He's a demon, isn't he?"

"No, and if there's only one thing you listen to at all from me, stay away from Zeke."

"But--"

"He will get you killed," Francis said firmly.

Lilly grunted and decided there was no use in protesting.

"Why'd you ask me to stay?"

"Training."

"I just trained, I learned how to defend myself. Maybe now you can tell me about my mom? Or demons? Something useful..." *like what Zeke is* Lilly thought.

"Throw some punches." Francis slid pads over his hands.

"No."

Francis held the pads up and stood in boxing stance.

"I'm going home." Lilly grabbed her backpack.

"Hey!" His voice was sharp and angry. "You agreed. We train." He pointed at her.

"To defend myself, not fight."

"To defend yourself you must fight."

"No, Francis. I don't want to fight."

"Did you hit those girls yesterday?"

She stopped and turned to him. "I mean, kinda."

"Then hit me." He held the pads up.

"Teach me about demons, about Zeke, the things that matter." She heaved her backpack over her shoulder.

"How do you expect to wield the sword?"

Lilly shrugged disinterestedly.

Francis let out a condescending laugh. "If you don't fight, you die, before you even get a chance to learn the things that matter *to you*. Now--"

"Fighting is stupid."

"Enjoy sulking, your mom would be so proud." He threw off the padded gloves.

"Shut up, Francis."

"Daughter sulks and dies at the hands of a demon."

She dropped her backpack and came charging at him. "Don't talk about her!"

"Why? I knew her better than you did."

Lilly's cheeks raged red. "You have no right, it's not fair."

"Life ain't fair, sweetheart. That's why you'll never know her."

That's when Lilly snapped. She decked Francis in the cheek, making a small cracking noise.

"Ha!" He wiggled his cheek.

She turned to leave. "I'm not doing this. It's stu--"

"You hit like a girl. Eva broke skin the first time she hit me." Francis bounced around on the balls of his feet. "Wanna know what that key goes to?" He pointed to Lilly's locket.

"What?"

"Throw a few more punches."

She shook her head.

"She left you something, but you'll never see it. Doesn't that just tick you off? All the things you'll never know about her, the things you can't even remem--"

Lilly let loose, punching his nose, then his gut, then his face, again and again. She had no idea what she was doing, just that she was angry enough to give fighting a try. She pictured Francis and Eva hanging out together at the park, Eva sharing her deepest of secrets with him. Sharing her favorite color, WHACK, listening to music, POW, hiking, POP, talking about Vin, SMACK. The tears started now. *They probably talked about me,* Lilly thought as she kicked at his shin, but it never hit. Francis grabbed her leg and she stood motionless trying not to fall over.

"Let go." She struggled and wiped the tears away.

"So you *can* fight. Now to do it without seeing red." Francis still held her leg, making sure she didn't kick him again.

She glared at him.

"How do your hands feel?"

She unclenched her fists and winced.

"That's what I thought." He dropped her leg slowly. "Come on." He beckoned her back to the mats.

Lilly didn't budge.

"Her favorite color was green." He paused. "Fighting was her favorite part, because girls weren't supposed to."

Lilly stepped onto the mat.

"Defiance, you have that in common."

Lilly let a grin escape her lips.

Francis took her hand. "Hold your thumb tighter here..."

They stayed at the gym practicing for another hour. Francis with blood on his face and Lilly with blood on her hands. He showed her how to punch and move her arm correctly and throw her body into a punch, and to always keep a hand at her chin to protect herself and keep her core tight.

Francis and Lilly leaned against the bleachers to catch their breath.

"See, not so bad, right?" Francis asked.

"Yeah, almost fun," she agreed. "So what's the key to?" She pointed to the locket around her neck.

"The key? Oh, I have no idea." Francis stood and laughed as she tried to trip him and threw her gloves at him.

All the while, Zeke sat on the roof watching through the skylight.

CHAPTER 19

"Life is not a problem to be solved, but a reality to be experienced."

Soren Kierkegaard

Francis let her put a little goo on her hands when they got home to settle some of the pain. But he had made it clear that she couldn't always use it, that eventually it would make her weak rather than let her get tough and strong.

Lilly only half listened, as she was glad to have it soothe her, at least for tonight. Her body ached all over and she wondered if there was a way to bathe in the stuff. Francis had probably picked up on it as he slid it away from her before he prepared dinner.

He asked her to stay and eat, but she declined. Lilly had hoped for a lot more time to herself by now, for the peace she never had at home. Somehow things had gotten more complicated than she ever imagined. A night to herself to think, or not think, was needed.

Walking through her doorway, she noticed Francis had warded her doorframe as well. The closing door echoed through the still apartment. She dropped her backpack at the door, opting to get to school early tomorrow and do homework then, since she *had* to get a good parking spot anyway.

Bending down she took her new cell phone from the front of her backpack; it had been on silent all day. She slid it into her pocket and checked the freezer.

Francis had asked her to please eat something before passing out. She knew he meant something healthy and sustainable, but a hot pocket would have to do. She sat down on her bed and took a peek at her phone.

There was a missed call from her dad and a few calls and texts from Vin.

Vin:

"THIS HOW IT'S GONNA BE NOW?"

"AT LEAST TELL US WHATS UP, HOW R U?"

" : - / "

Lilly grimaced and closed her eyes tight. For the first time in a long time, she felt her heart twist. Behind her eyelids she pictured their house. Vin, Mom, Dad, Emma, and Lilly, all sitting in the living room playing rummy. Happy and laughing. She opened her eyes and a tear escaped. Her vision was a lie, Mom was gone, Dad was ten years older with burden, and Lilly and her siblings were much older, no longer together.

Her eyes wandered around the apartment, at the nothingness. The tears came more freely. "I can't go back, not now." She croaked and fell back on the bed. Lilly fell asleep crying, without taking a bite of anything.

Lilly had no idea what was chasing her, only that she couldn't run fast enough. The dark figures terrified her, making her heart race. Every time she looked back, they were right on her heels and out in front of her everything was a fog. A terrible high-pitched screaming cry came from one of them. Lilly turned to see what was happening and that's when she started falling.

"Up and at 'em."

Lilly slammed back into bed. She opened her eyes to the dogs licking her salty face and Francis smiling down at her.

"How'd you get in?" she grumbled.

"Apparently you left the door unlocked. Not the best practice. C'mon then." Francis motioned her up.

She groaned, turning on her side, "The sun isn't even up."

Cuff and Link stopped licking and ran at the corner of the room growling and barring their teeth.

"Make them stop, Francis. Ughhh." She pulled the pillow over her head.

"'Hey!" He snapped at the dogs, they ran to his side. "Get up Lilly, it's time to train." He flipped the mattress on its side, throwing Lilly out of bed.

"You're outta your mind!" Lilly unsteadily got to her feet and threw a finger in Francis's face. "I sleep, I sleep at five AM!" She shouted after seeing the time.

"You run at five AM." Francis clipped the leashes onto the dogs' collars and handed them to Lilly. Before she had a chance to argue he was out the front door. She looked back and forth between the dogs, then back at the bed. In one lazy motion, she dropped the leashes and fell back into bed, but the dogs were on her in an instant, crying and lapping at her face.

"No!" They howled now. "OK, OK!"

Francis was smiling, chipper, and jogging in place next to the front stoop. "Beautiful morning for a run."

"It's freezing."

"Best time to run." With that he was off and the dogs were fast behind him, forcing Lilly to run with them, or as close to with them as she was capable of.

"I run at least five miles a day. Keeps the mind at peace," he explained, "it'll help you outrun the slower demons."

"And... the... faster... ones?" The cold air made it hard for Lilly to breath, let alone talk.

Francis shrugged. "Hopefully you'll outsmart them, fight, or you'll have help. The fun part is deciding what to do."

By the end of it Lilly was hardly jogging. The dogs were making her keep going. Francis was out of sight, but the dogs knew their way back.

"I never... thought... I'd make it... five miles." Lilly smiled, collapsing next to Francis on the steps outside the apartment. He had been waiting for her for a while now.

"You did three." He handed her a bottle of water.

"Oh, uh..." she groaned. "It felt like ten."

"You'll get there." Francis patted her shoulder. She shoved him back, but he didn't budge; he just laughed at her.

"This is gonna kill me." She shook her head, smiling.

"Only if you let it. Meet me at the park right after school." He clicked twice for the dogs, who obediently followed him in after giving Lilly a few good thank you kisses.

"You're smiling more already, it's the endorphins!" He laughed before the door shut behind him.

Lilly shook her head. She drew in a deep breath, slowly exhaled, and took in the quiet morning around her.

"Hey, so what's up, are you not working anymore or something?" Kathy sat down across from Lilly at lunch.

Lilly was spacing out, watching an exchange between Zeke and another kid.

"Hello, Donna Day Dream!" Erica laughed.

160

"What?"

"Did you quit, or something? Mildred said your dad called saying you couldn't work?" Kathy asked.

"Oh, the grocery store, I mean, yeah…" Lilly imagined Francis called pretending to be her dad.

The whole group, except Jen, was waiting for an explanation. Or maybe Jen was paying attention, just pretending not to.

"My parents, they were really upset I got a job. They want me to concentrate on my studies. You know for college, and…" she paused and smiled, "and I'm training for a marathon with my mom next year. Francis, our neighbor, is helping me train." Lilly's lie made her happier than she had anticipated.

"Oh that's so cool! I wish my parents would do something like that with me," Erica chimed in.

"Yeah or discourage me from working," Kathy laughed. "We should run together, with your mom. Before work Saturday?"

"Umm, well, my parents are actually out of town this weekend."

"Oh, even better, let's move the party to your place Friday!" Yup, Jen was listening.

"Yea!" Dawn exclaimed.

"Well-"

"That'd be cool," Kathy agreed.

"Then it's settled, Lilly's place after school tomorrow."

"TGIF! Can't wait!"

They stood at the sound of the bell and everyone was gone before Lilly could protest.

Lilly was avoiding walking through the smoke corner, not wanting to rehash the experience. She took the longer way through the Tech Ed wing and out the other end of the building. There was a wood shop, a metal shop, and one classroom had a garage with a car shop so the gear heads could work on their cars and get school credit for it. Not a bad deal to get credit for something you love and plan to do anyway.

Lilly strode down the empty hall to the outside door and swung it open. There stood Zeke leaning against a tree, smoking a cigarette. His hair was falling over his face today; he must have run out of gel. Lilly huffed and quickly turned towards the trailers, but Zeke caught up with her in no time.

"Wanna skip with me?" Zeke asked, placing his hand on the small of her back.

Her body tingled at his touch and she straightened her posture. She smiled; she did want to skip with him. There was nothing more boring to her than History class and she was sure

Zeke had answers for her that Francis didn't. But when the tingly thrill of his touch faded, pains shot through her wrists.

"Why?" She stopped and turned to face him.

"Huh?"

"Why skip with me?"

Zeke stuttered, surprised by her bluntness. "I mean, w-w-why not?"

The pains in her wrists quickly slowed to a dying, dull, pulse. "Why doesn't Francis like you? He told me to stay away from you, that you'd get me killed."

Zeke went white as a ghost. He rubbed his neck and looked around uncomfortably. "I mean…"

"Well, what are you? He said you're not an angel or demon, so what are you?"

Zeke's face regained some color, and then he burst out laughing. He didn't stop and for the first time in the past few days Lilly thought that this whole angel and demon talk was actually her going nuts like her mom.

"I'm losing it. This place made me crazy," She strutted away with her face in her hands, embarrassed.

Zeke stopped laughing and caught up to her. "Wait, I'm sorry, don't go to class. I'll explain." He took her hand. "You're not crazy. Francis doesn't trust me because I'm not angel or demon… I'm *both* and that's unpredictable."

The bell rang and voices of teachers echoed from around the corner. "Come on." He nodded again towards the parking lot.

She was finally getting answers from someone.

Before she had a chance to think about it, Zeke and Lilly were in his car jetting out of the parking lot.

"So he told you then, what you are?" Zeke asked as he put on his left turn signal.

Lilly's eyes narrowed, staring at him.

"Hey, that's fine, don't trust me, but you probably shouldn't have gotten in a car with me, then."

"He said I'm the Keeper of the sword, the Ferryman. So, what does that make you, not-angel-not-demon?" They had barely gone a mile and Zeke was already pulling into his driveway.

"Half Life," he said simply and put the car in park.

"What?"

But Zeke got out and didn't answer her. He stepped towards her side of the car to open her door, then stopped himself and made for the front door of the house. Lilly jumped out and followed him.

The front door swung open on its own.

"Skipping?" Skoal's voice was firm.

"Yeah, whatever, I know." Zeke brushed by him. "Skoal this is Lilly, Lilly this is Skoal."

"Hi, uh, nice to meet you." Lilly put out her hand, but Skoal leaned in and hugged her.

"Wonderful, Lilly!" Skoal pulled back from the hug. His eyes were a bright green. "What are you doing skipping class with this knucklehead?" He closed the front door behind them and eyed Zeke.

"Skoal, please, privacy."

Skoal snorted and vanished from the room.

Lilly's jaw dropped. "He--"

"He's a Manipulator. And he's happy to show it off." Zeke sunk into the couch and threw his feet up on the giant hardwood coffee table.

"Manipulator? Is he your dad? How does that make you a Half Life?" Lilly questioned. She bit her tongue as she watched Zeke's face contort uncomfortably. "I'm sorry. I hate people asking me all kinds of questions. I didn't mean to make you uncomfortable." She sat down in a chair catty-corner to him. "Francis hasn't really explained much. It's just exciting to talk to someone who *knows*."

"He's a strange one."

Lilly took a look around the room in the hopes that Zeke would offer up some answers in the silence. The walls

165

were almost entirely covered in bookshelves. Not all of them bore books, but the ones that did had books of every age and size. Some were huge anthologies, tattered and falling apart. Others looked brand new, but still worn as if every book that they owned had been read through in its entirety.

"How did Skoal disappear?" Lilly asked, her back to him.

"It's called Fading, a simple manipulation of time and space."

One wall had a giant glass case filled with ancient weapons from floor to ceiling. Lilly walked over to it, not letting Zeke see her surprise. Swords, daggers, a bow and arrow, throwing stars, a strange looking double-ended dagger that Zeke said was a *haladie*. A spear that nearly reached the ceiling rested on the side of the glass case. But Lilly remained clueless about most of the other items in the case.

"Cool." She held back the *holy cow* ringing in her head.

Some of the shelves without books had small jars filled with dust, herbs, or weird things like crows feet. Most were clear, but there were colored pots with corks in the tops, unmarked; Lilly wished she knew what was in them. All the decorations appeared to be ancient artifacts, paintings, or tools dug up from centuries before.

"A Half Life is..." Zeke started, "in life we might be good people, or bad people, but in the moment of death a Half Life does something to redeem or damn themselves. When our soul leaves our body, we're met with both an angel and a demon." There was a dull twinkle in his eyes. "They fight over your soul, Lilly. Until... Pax." He recalled the day on the battlefield and cringed. "They reach a stalemate. Neither angel nor demon is able to take your soul. It's the most painful thing I've ever known." Zeke stood. "Your soul is torn to pieces, then put back together, with a new body. A body given to you by both angel and demon... and yet you're still human." He tapped his heart.

Lilly sat down again, stunned.

"Well, now you know." He grabbed a deck of cards from one of the shelves. "We're not to be trusted, too evil to be good for you." He tried to laugh. "You know how to play poker?"

―――――――

"What time is it?" Lilly had been absorbed in their game. She had convinced him to play rummy after a pitiful game of poker.

Zeke held out his watch. It read 2:30pm.

"Shoot, I have to go." Lilly stepped towards the door.

Zeke followed. "I'll give you a ride back to your car."

Lilly thought. What would Francis do if he knew she was with Zeke? "No, no, we're not too far from school. Thanks though." She jetted out the door.

Zeke watched from the window as Lilly jogged down the street towards the school. Skoal appeared behind him.

"She seems very nice."

"She is." Zeke let the curtain fall shut.

Skoal stood in front of him, arms crossed. "Are you prepared to *damn* her?" His face was stern with anger.

Zeke disappeared.

"Run. You always run when it gets too tough."

CHAPTER 20

"Never confuse a single defeat with a final defeat."

F. Scott Fitzgerald

"Hey, sorry, Francis. I lost track of time and then I got lost."

It was well after three o'clock when Lilly reached the park. She had forgotten where exactly it was and had to circle around for the entrance. When she pulled up Francis was tossing a stick to the dogs and appeared to be casually talking to himself. "We've been waiting." He looked down to his left at nothing; the dogs were to his right.

Lilly stared and then laughed uncomfortably.

"Well, we better get started." She tossed her backpack off her shoulder and rested it against a tree trunk. "What's first? Uppercuts?"

Francis stared skeptically at her enthusiasm. He shook it off and turned to his left again. "I want you to meet Iris."

As Francis spoke, a short, trim woman appeared beside him; looking closer she had tiny wings and was very toned. Iris had short blond hair, with skin so light it was almost yellow, and her face always held a smile.

Iris didn't stay at Francis's side very long. It was apparent she had trouble staying in one place at all or holding her attention on one thing. One moment she was in front of Lilly, then beside Francis, then out in the middle of the field watching the geese waddle around. Her feet never seemed to move; the only sign of movement was a very faint blur from one location to the next.

She was in front of Lilly again. "Glad 'ta officially meet ya, Lilly." Her voice was hasty, nasally, and high pitched. Her body twitched or buzzed like a humming bird, moving so fast she appeared to be moving slowly.

"You too, Iris." Lilly couldn't help but smile at the sight of her. Iris was like a pleasantly curious child.

"Iris is our greatest messenger. She comes with a message and gifts."

"Well, maybe not the greatest." Iris blushed. "Just try my best." First she was at Francis's left, then to his right by the dogs. Her words were so fast they too were almost just a buzz of jumbled syllables. "That's all any of us can do, try our best." She gave Francis's shoulder a friendly punch. "Anyhoo, the message…"

Iris stood before Lilly as still as she could, her eyes closed and she exhaled. She looked right into Lilly's eyes as she slowed her speech. "Absorb all knowledge of my world, the world below, and where they meet. You'll find the sword at your mother's heart. Question everyone, no one is all good or all wicked." Iris tilted her head. "You look just like your mother."

Lilly grimaced. *I hate it, why,* Lilly thought.

"No, no, it's good, it's good." Iris lifted Lilly's head. She stared into Lilly's eyes and she felt her pain, the cell that held her. Iris's empathy warmed Lilly. After a moment, Iris smiled wide. "Oh! The gifts."

She whipped a dagger from her robes, nearly slashing Lilly's side, but she jumped, avoiding the double-edged blade.

Behind Iris, Francis stood holding back a chuckle. He was used to Iris, but watching her with a human was a joy he had not seen in some time.

"This is Sabriel, your substitute for the Ferryman." Iris slid it into a dark leather sheath and held it out for Lilly to take.

Slowly, as if Iris might take it and thrash it around once more, Lilly took it. She slid it from the sheath and held it clumsily. Iris grazed her hand over the dagger and it glowed blue, then orange.

"Take it with you everywhere, it's your key to the other worlds. Only you and a select few can see it." As Iris spoke she took just the sheath from Lilly, unbuckled Lilly's belt and slid the sheath into place on it.

Lilly looked quizzically from Iris to the dagger in her hands. It seemed to shimmer and fade, but it was there.

171

Lilly opened her mouth to speak, but Iris clapped her hands together.

"Gift two! My favorite!" Iris shifted back and forth on the balls of her feet and shook excitedly.

Lilly's eyes went wide and she gasped. Quickly she slid the dagger in the sheath at her side to keep it out of Iris's grasp. Francis openly laughed this time. Lilly turned to stare him down, but Iris's hands shot up in front of her face. She stared wide-eyed at the backs of Iris's hands.

"Hmm..." Iris lowered her hands and took an old skin pouch from her side. She dashed a glowing liquid on each of her hands, and then uttered, "Cernitis omnia, bonum et malum. Statera pace, statera pace." Without warning, she thrust her palms over Lilly's eyes and repeated her words.

Lilly tried to back away, but suddenly someone stood behind her, and her hands were firmly held at her side. She panicked and twisted around, but it was no use. The sticky glowing concoction from the canteen was in and around her eyes. It stung and smelled of honey.

"What's wrong with you! Francis, help!" She threw her head back and found it rested against a chest. Iris, at the same time, dropped her hands away.

"Numquam in eodem," Iris's squeaky voice whispered.

"Sorry, kid," Francis's voice emerged from behind her. Lilly elbowed him without giving it a second thought.

As a few pain-induced tears surfaced, the stinging stopped and Lilly found she was able to carefully open her eyes. The liquid had already dried and began turning to dust. She lifted her hand to rub her eyes and sooth the ache, but Iris's hand stopped her.

"Hold on, close your eyes."

Lilly obeyed.

Iris took a deep breath and exhaled over Lilly's eyes. The dust fell away with her breath and slowly Lilly opened one eye at a time.

Iris stood in front of her, but this was a different Iris. Lilly could see her movement clearly now, almost in slow motion, and her skin was golden, glowing. She had small bright white wings tucked behind her so that they were barely visible. Her feet had tiny fluttery wings as well. Lilly's eyebrows furrowed and she tried to step back, but she ran into Francis.

Turning she found Francis with a nervous smile. His face appeared younger. He too had a glow about him, but his was very dim. Backing away from Francis, her head tilted up to see his wings, or the shadow of wings. They were a light

173

outline, barely glowing, but they towered over him in a resting position.

Feeling sick, she looked from Francis then back to Iris.

Lilly had trusted Iris, because she trusted Francis. Enraged, she punched Francis square in the jaw, exactly how he had taught her just the day before. It clearly stung as he closed his eyes and rolled his jaw around a few times.

"You learn quickly," Francis rubbed his jaw.

"Tell someone before you throw magic goo in their damned eyes," Lilly shouted.

"Good luck training," Iris squeaked delightedly and vanished, leaving Francis to deal with Lilly.

"It only works on unknowing eyes," Francis said plainly. "Now, what do you see?" Francis crossed his arms over his chest. Lilly had scarcely taken her eyes off him.

"You look younger."

Francis scoffed.

"Wings." She stepped closer, reaching out.

"Go ahead." He nodded.

She went to touch his wings, but her hand went right through them. Francis made a sound as if it hurt. "But…"

"They're not real. Not anymore." He paced towards the woods. It would start getting dark soon and they still had an entire lesson. "My wings are just a memory, a reminder that I

174

was once an angel and chose to live a life as a human. We are called Jumpers."

"Why?" Lilly followed close behind.

"Because we jump to earth and choose not to use our wings. They disintegrate in the fall. When we hit the ground we're like you, human. Sometimes a few of our powers linger."

"No, I mean why did you jump, Francis?"

His face contorted uncomfortably. "Come on, let's use that dagger."

"Tell me at some point at least?" Lilly wondered what would possess an angel to leave what she imagined to be a perfect life.

"One day." He took Sabriel from her belt and rested it on his palm for Lilly to see. "Sabriel here," he nodded to the dagger, "was forged during the same age as the Ferryman. There are few like it and most are locked away. In the wrong hands, this simple knife could destroy the entire world." His voice was stern. He stared at Lilly to make sure she understood.

Lilly nodded.

"Sabriel has two edges. The thicker side," he pointed to the edge that had Runes down it that glowed red-orange, "will take you too far, to Limbo and beyond." Lilly looked confused so he added, "The layers of Hell, Lilly."

She nodded.

"The thin side will take you to Abditus."

"Heaven?"

"No. Abditus is… Abditus. Heaven is protected; you can't simply go there. Not without…" Francis shook his head. "Let's get through the basics--"

"Why protect Heaven and leave Hell wide open?"

"Hell invites anyone to its miseries. Don't think entering Hell would be easy, either." Lilly nodded, letting him go on. "So, Hell," He pointed to the thick side. "And Abditus." He pointed to the thin side of the blade.

He looked up and waited for Lilly to confirm she understood.

"Then to seal it." He placed his thumb on the very end of the hilt and pinched the tip of the dagger carefully between the fingers on his other hand. He swung the dagger in a vertical sweeping motion. "Seal it with the fuller."

"The what?"

"The groove in the center, drag that against the tear. You always have to seal it." He dropped the dagger down away from their eyes and handed it to Lilly. "Always."

"Got it, leave a gaping hole in the universe whenever possible."

Francis's eyes narrowed.

"I can follow directions, Francis." She lifted the dagger, the thicker side down. "Now, what do I cut to get to this Abditus you speak of?" She thrashed the dagger around jokingly, cutting a few slits in the air in front of her.

Her jaw dropped, it was as if someone had painted a realistic landscape in its entirety and she cut their beautiful canvas painting. Behind the 'slashed painting' poured out red bubbling lava and seven black scaly fingers equipped with pointy, marble-like nails.

"AH! No, no, no, no, no!" Francis bellowed in alarm. He snatched the dagger from Lilly who was still in awe, unable to look anywhere else. Hastily he held the dagger on its side and drew the fuller back and forth over the slashes Lilly had made. The black fingers darted back into Hell.

It closed up just in time to hide a yellow wandering eye and snap off a piece of now igneous rock that crashed to the earth, shattering. There were no remnants of the other world now, just air.

"This," he pointed, "is not a toy." He spoke slowly, gasping. He glared at her, before reluctantly handing it back. "She's going to damn us all," he muttered, staring at the sky.

"She's going to damn us all," she mimicked.

"Which side to Abditus?"

Lilly held the thin side down.

"Good. Now gently, very gently, drag it through the air, anywhere, anywhere are all, with intent, from shoulders to knees."

Lilly followed his instructions, mockingly.

"Gently." Francis sweated uncomfortably.

"Gently," Lilly mimicked as she finished the cut.

This time the slash in the earthly canvas just showed gray behind it.

"Let's go." Francis picked up his own bag and brushed the two curtain-like pieces of the woods apart. He ushered her in. Lilly grabbed her backpack and stepped into Abditus without a thought. Francis followed. "Close it."

Cuff and Link sat on the other side of the slash, wagging their tails and whining. "The dogs--"

"They're not allowed here. Close it."

Not wanting to argue, Lilly imitated what Francis did just a minute before. She watched as the fuller closed up the break in the curtain. They stood in a dark nothingness now; she imagined it was much like standing in the vastness of space.

Then something very strange happened. A few words dashed by. Handwritten words floated above her head, "*wish Mom and Dad understood...*" The image of a test with a 'D' written in red ink floated next to it.

Lilly looked up higher and saw other images, words, and see-through glowing beings she decided were spirits, all floating around everywhere as far as she could see. Some were slow and some were so fast they were just a blur.

Then she saw them, big beautiful gray-white wings at least fifteen feet wide. They flapped twice then stopped, leaving the angel staring down, hundreds of feet above her. The dark haired angel smiled down at Lilly. Her eyes were green, her skin a pale glistening brown, and the angel was slowly getting bigger as she descended.

"What is this place?" Lilly stared.

"The world between the worlds. It's how the supernatural get around so quickly, it's where we hide. A no man's land. Angels can fly around the whole world in one human second twice, thanks to Abditus."

"Wow..." Lilly gulped. "And the words?" She pointed at a few jumbled words.

"The truth behind telepathy. Most people leave their minds open and their thoughts exist here in the spiritual world.

True telepaths know the secrets of Abditus. This is how I hear your thoughts."

Lilly watched as the spirits and winged creatures above them slowed and began watching Lilly and Francis.

"Why are they staring?"

"It's not every day a human walks into Abditus, Lilly."

"Gabriel!" shouted the brown-skinned angel, except her shout was like a light jazz song turned on high.

The beautiful angel landed gracefully in front of them. She was so tall, Lilly had to lean her head back to see her face. She had a sword at her side and her robes were lined with purple. Another angel, a blonde-haired masculine creature who Lilly guessed was Gabriel, landed next to her. He was even taller than the other angel and easily the most attractive being she had ever seen. They both wore what looked like some sort of casual robes mixed with a light chain mail that wasn't quite metal.

"Lilly!" Gabriel embraced her. "Francis." Gabriel turned to Francis. They fist bumped, exploded it and then embraced. "Finally!"

"You received Iris's gifts." The other angel nodded. She held a large wooden staff of very light, almost white wood. On the top rested a purple glowing orb that drew Lilly's attention. She just wanted to stare at it close up, and maybe touch it.

"Yes." Francis turned to Lilly, who jumped and leaned away from the newcomers and their orbs. "Lilly, this is Archangel Suriel the Merciful, and Archangel Gabriel the Robust."

Lilly did an odd, uncomfortable curtsy.

Suriel beamed. "I'm just so happy!" Her jazz voice echoed and she threw her arms wide open. A burst of light shot out from her staff and suddenly as far as Lilly could see was light, bright, and beautiful.

"Calm yourself, Suriel." Gabriel rested his hand on her shoulder.

Lilly's mouth was wide with a gaping smile, watching the world brighten around them.

"I'm just excited," Suriel squealed.

"It's ok," Lilly assured her.

"Well let's see it then, the training." Gabriel nodded at Lilly. He leaned on his staff expectantly. His was all white with an orb of pure white light at the top.

"Here, in front of…" Lilly trailed off. Angels and spirits unknown had been gathering since Lilly and Francis emerged from their own world to theirs.

"Good thinking, yup, we'll need a ring," Francis pointed into the now bright emptiness. A beam of light glowed from his hand and the ground turned pearly white.

"I'll take it from here!" Suriel lifted her staff. She tapped and flicked it towards the pearly white floor. Greek columns appeared here and there, and stone walls with archways surfaced, circling around the floor forming a coliseum, with rows and rows of seats that reached so high they were lost in the gray cloudy nothingness of Abditus. With each dash of her staff something new appeared as if it was being built in fast forward.

Lilly watched in wonderment as the other angels joined in adding an obstacle course, punching bags, weights, boxing gloves, a padded ring. Then to the coliseum itself they added torches, statues of beings and animals, tiny fine carvings, flags, tapestries, and so much more than she could take in.

Am I high? Lilly thought. She watched as the thought rose from her head and the words floated into the air. She jumped and grabbed at them but her hands went right through them.

Gabriel's laugh was so deep it shook Lilly. He bent down a few feet to her, placing his arm around her and smiled. "You might learn to keep your thoughts to yourself."

Lilly wiggled uncomfortably. She would have been happy to have her thoughts to herself, but the whole point of Abditus seemed to be to take away your privacy. Her nose wrinkled and she nudged his shoulder to get away from him.

Go away, she thought, actually happy to see the words rise into the air this time hoping that it would make Gabriel leave her alone. But he just laughed again; she felt it shake through her. "You will learn." Pulling her in so tight and lifting her up off the ground to his height with one arm, she realized his strength was so great she couldn't even wiggle this time.

Gabriel light kissed her forehead and rubbed her should, then grinned and put her down. He enjoyed her discomfort just as much as Francis did, releasing her only when she calmed down.

"You will learn." Gabriel winked.

Gabriel stepped forward into the center of the coliseum where Francis waited and tapped his staff against the floor. It rippled through the entire arena, shaking it. "Seats!" His voice echoed. "Let's show our new Keeper how to keep the peace!"

Thousands upon thousands of angels were gathered, with every color wings, some smaller, some larger. Some had two or three sets of wings, a few had more sets of eyes than Lilly could count. One angel appeared to have three heads, one

183

of a man, one of a lion, and one of an eagle. But Lilly blinked, and it was just a winged man. She must have imagined it.

The angels' cheers and applause were so loud Lilly closed her eyes, trying to ease her senses, but she still felt the applause and overwhelming number of beings around her. She tried her hardest to keep her thoughts inside her head, but she wouldn't open her eyes to see if they had escaped.

A hand pressed against her back.

"Francis."

"They're very excited."

She opened her eyes and stared at him blankly.

"It is a bit overwhelming, I agree, but they haven't had a human to entertain them in a decade."

"I'm not good at this, Francis."

"That's why we're here, so you can become good at it."

It was a silent agreement that they weren't just talking about her physical training, but also how she acted around others. The angels didn't even have to be excited to see her or make noise to make her uncomfortable, all they had to do was look at her or pay attention to her. It was like the first day of school all over again, everyone staring and whispering about her.

"You can do no wrong. They've already accepted you because of your parents. You must do what you think you can't." Francis pushed her forward.

Lilly shook her head and he stopped.

"I'll go, let me do it," Lilly said and she stepped into the coliseum herself. Taking in every detail, she took the long walk to the center of the ring, circling to see every inch of it. The architecture was beautiful, impossible for just a few minutes of work, so she touched it to find it was in fact real.

As her eyes met each angel in the stands, Lilly set a smile on her face. They were happy simply because Lilly was there, she had to remember that, the least she could do was try to smile. Reaching the center of the arena, her circling came to a stop at seven throne-like stone seats raised above the ring, but on the lowest level of the coliseum. Five seats were filled, two empty.

Francis was just a few steps behind her the whole way. When she stopped, he stopped at her side. They looked to the seven seats together.

"Gabriel and Suriel, you met," Frances stated. Both angels smiled at her. "Jophiel, Chamuel, and Raziel. They are the Archangels." Francis pointed to each one.

Jophiel had a scruffy red beard with very short hair on the sides of his head and longer wavy hair on top. He carried a smaller staff that glowed yellow at the crest and had lots of little decorative carvings down it. Jophiel only met Lilly's eyes for a brief moment when his name was called, but his eyes quickly found other things to look at.

Chamuel was the only one who looked annoyed, almost angry. The corners of her lips barely pursed a smiled and she stared directly into Lilly's eyes, making it hard for Lilly to keep eye contact with her very long. Chamuel's red hair curved around her left cheekbone and was all buzzed on the right side of her head. Her staff had a red orb.

Raziel openly waved at Lilly, his curly black hair bouncing at his shoulders. Like the others he was in excellent shape, but Raziel was the only one who didn't find it necessary to wear a shirt at all and was clearly more muscular than the others. He wore long baggy gray pants like a genie. Lilly wondered how he didn't trip over them. His chest was covered in tattoos of Runes, ancient writing, and tiny animal silhouettes. One large Rune was tattooed over his heart with smaller ones circling it. His staff rested on the ground under his feet, the tiny orb in it glowing orange.

"Who are the other two seats for?" Lilly asked.

Before Francis had a chance to answer, Gabriel shouted, "Michael and Raphael! Maybe one of these days they will join us."

The Archangels laughed, except for Chamuel, who appeared even more annoyed, if that was possible.

"Lighten up Cha," Raziel's deep voiced echoed.

"Let's get on with this, Raz." Chamuel nodded to Lilly who again turned away at her gaze.

Gabriel motioned to Francis.

"We'll start with some foot work." Francis dashed through the two rows of tires. Next he jumped over a few hurdles, and then he dodged in and out of a number of punching bags. It ended with him sprinting in and out of a ladder.

Francis jogged to Lilly's side. "Ten rounds. Go." He motioned.

"Ten?" Lilly scoffed.

"Don't disappoint, they're counting on you being a good Keeper." He winked.

"And when I'm not?"

"Not a chance, you'll be amazing like your mother."

Lilly looked around again at the angels circled around her. She focused on Raziel, then Suriel, who were giving her the most pleasant vibes.

Reaching to take off her jacket, she looked down and watched her legs disappear in a purple cloud of smoke. It engulfed her, and when it dissipated she wore black three-

187

quarter-length leggings with purple accents and a purple tank top. Both had a small cursive "$\mathcal{A}$" embroidered on them.

Suriel squealed with joy.

Before Lilly could give herself another chance at doubt, she dashed to the start of the course. Her first round through she tripped twice in the tires, leaving black rubber marks on her shins. Each time she winced, but pushed herself back up, determined to be as good as her mom.

She ran into each hurdle with a slap against the top of her feet, knocking a few over. The punching bags weren't as bad; she took them slower and only brushed them. The ladder was by far the easiest, but she had seen people use these before and assumed Francis would give her more complicated foot movements at some point.

As she circled for round two, she opened her mouth to say she couldn't, but Francis shook his head and pushed her forward. "You're amazing, keep going, you've got this!"

And the angels cheered. Gabriel flicked his staff toward the hurdles and they flung back into place.

Round two, Lilly took the tires slower and she didn't fall at all. She stumbled, but she didn't fall. The hurdles again were just as bad, and the punching bags and ladder she took faster. Francis urged her on and the angels cheers continued for four rounds.

But at round five, Lilly hit her first hurdle hard and this time she fell and stayed on the ground with her head hung low. She hadn't made it over a single one without hitting it.

It felt like an hour she crouched there begging her feet and legs to stop throbbing before she felt Francis's hand.

"Get up." There was no sympathy in his voice.

The angels' cheers had quieted some.

"I can't, I can't do this. I don't want to."

"Who taught you *can't*? It's a silly human word, *can't* is just a synonym for won't."

"Lower the hurtles, then, so I can learn."

"No. What will you do when there is a demon on your heels? Ask them to run slower?"

Lilly raised her head, ready to shout at him for the insanity of it. *How many times do I have to hurt myself to teach him I can't?*

She looked up and saw her thoughts, *"...hurt myself... I can't"*. Her face contorted, but not from the pain. Pushing herself off the ground, Lilly stood the hurdle back up herself.

"How then?"

"You're jumping too soon. Let's make it only three." He nodded to the Archangels.

Raziel flicked his wrist and every other hurdle disappeared. The angels grew quiet.

189

"Remember, you are good enough and it's ok to ask for help." Francis used his foot to scratch lines in the dirt. "Jump here."

Lilly nodded.

"Lead each jump with your right leg, raise your knee high," Francis showed her. "Tuck your right foot in more, and then bring your back left foot up to your armpit when you jump."

Francis took a step back and Lilly took a deep breath. Jumping where she was told, Lilly bounded over her first hurtle effortlessly. The angelic crowed cheered wildly. Lilly took the next two just grazing the last enough to shake it.

Looking to Francis she beamed from ear to ear. He smiled back and motioned for her to finish the course. After ten rounds, Lilly dashed over to Francis. She still hit many of the hurdles but not nearly as hard and didn't knock too many over.

"What's next?" Lilly jogged in place in front of Francis.

"Now you're excited?" Francis grinned, rubbing her head, purposefully messing up her hair.

"Hey, hey!" Lilly shooed him. "A cheering section and personal trainer in the arts of demon hunting kind of helps." She fixed her hair as she spoke.

"I would imagine." Francis went for her hair again, but she dodged him.

They ran through some boxing drills, punches, and defensive moves. Then Francis made her run around the perimeter of the coliseum twice.

Jophiel swooped down next to Francis and they spoke while Lilly ran. Slowly, one by one, the angels left. They had to get back to their work; they had already abandoned their duties for far too long. Jophiel, Suriel, and Francis were the only ones who stayed.

Suriel dashed her staff around to make a sitting area for them, a large dry erase board, and a desk with a pen and paper. Mindlessly, Suriel made purple designs across the seats, lavender flowers sprouted from the ground, and a little purple flowing stream through the coliseum. Jophiel crossed his staff over hers. His face was airy, but serious.

Suriel stopped, but not before changing Jophiel's robes a bright boysenberry.

Francis motioned Lilly to come in from her run. She trotted back to them and Suriel handed her a large goblet of water. As she drank, more water appeared in its place. Lilly's eyes grew wide as she drank more just to watch it happen again.

"Amazing!"

Suriel smiled at her exuberance.

"Jophiel will be leading you in Demonology today." Suriel motioned for her to sit.

Lilly joined them. Jophiel swung his hand through the air and 'Demonology' appeared at the top of the board.

Lilly scratched it at the top of her paper.

"Just as there are seven Archangels, there are seven demons. They call themselves the Princes--"

"And Princess." Suriel cut Jophiel off.

"And Princess of Hell. Thoth, Prince of sloth, head of the demon Reapers." As he spoke it appeared on the board. He sat back, motionless.

Lilly scribbled away.

"Bile, Prince of gluttony, creator of sorrows. Azazel, Prince of pride, Gate Keeper of Hell. Leviathan, Prince of envy, maker of pain. Mommon, Prince of greed, Head of Hell's book keepers. And finally, Lucifer and Lilith, King and Queen of Hell, emissaries of wrath and lust."

Lilly scribbled away, hardly hearing him, just continuing to look up at the board. As she wrote the last two, she looked up, saw no more, and then stared down at her paper. Mindlessly she underlined Lilith a few times.

"You must know who these seven are. They are the only organized evil that Hell has, the only real threat to this

192

world." Jophiel's voice grew heated. "They coordinate the Penthus', spirits of grief, from collecting good sorrows. They stop guardian angels from protecting their marks, prevent the Virtues from performing miracles, stop messengers in their tracks, put holes in the Earth's first line of defense, the Powers, and--" Francis cleared his throat, and Jophiel stopped immediately.

"...We will come back to them." Jophiel uttered as his helpless eyes wandered to the sky.

"Go over one type of demon, and a Half Life. Then we can go." Francis looked down at his watch. It had two watch faces on it, but one ticked more slowly than the other.

Lilly's face went red when he said Half Life.

"Zeke is a Half Life," Francis said.

As they explained a Half Life in detail Lilly jotted down notes, trying not to make eye contact with them, for fear they would know where she really learned of a Half Life and Pax.

"A Half Life is contracted by angels and demons to commit acts that they cannot on earth, the end result being the Half Life finding their place in the afterlife."

Lilly continued to scribble notes.

"What demon would you like to learn of?"

Lilly shrugged, not knowing what there even was to learn.

"Oh! A Nightmare, they're everywhere," Suriel suggested.

"A *Nightmare?*"

"What dreams are made of." Jophiel flicked his wrist and 'Nightmare' appeared on the board.

A creature began sketching itself out on the board. It resembled a Gargoyle, but was short and fat like a bulldog. Its back legs ended at hooves and its front legs were claw-like. Its wings looked too small to haul the solid little creature around, instead only allowing it to hop from place to place. Its snarly grin had five or six sharp little fangs popping out under its wrinkly mouth.

"Let's see your dagger."

Lilly took it from the sheath and handed it to Jophiel.

"Nightmares lurk everywhere, giving anyone weak minded enough night terrors and--"

"If you're strong, a nightmare can't hurt you?"

"If your guard is down, you let negativity in. Then you're susceptible to them, yes," Suriel replied. "Imagine an open wound. If you don't clean it, medicate it, and cover it then it's likely to get infected and get worse, maybe even kill you, right?"

"Right."

"If your mind is weak, open to negativity, it is open to more negativity and unhappiness. Leave it open and you're likely to get infected, by Nightmares."

Lilly wrinkled her nose at the thought of an *infected mind*. An image of a rotting zombie brain floated above her. Suriel and Francis both chuckled.

"Protecting your mind will help you with that too."

"I can't learn that fast enough!"

"That is another lesson, the art of Lito," Jophiel replied as he held the dagger straight in front of him with the blade facing out. "Hold it so, placing your thumb on the end of the pommel."

Lilly took the dagger and did exactly that. As her thumb pressed against the end a dull blue beam shot out from the edge of the blade and circled over her knuckles to her thumb. Startled, she dropped her thumb from the end and the beam disappeared.

"Don't let go," Jophiel told her.

Again, she pressed her thumb against the pommel, this time the beam crossed over her knuckles solid and a shade darker.

"The dagger," Francis started, "will help you channel your abilities, until you can do without it."

"My abilities?" Lilly questioned, but no one offered an explanation.

"When a Nightmare comes near, punch it right between the eyes." Jophiel showed off a quick jab.

"That's it?"

"Yes." Suriel nodded.

Jophiel was already wandering off. His wings expanded and he leapt into the air.

"Until next time." Suriel half squatted and leapt into the air herself.

Lilly was left with Francis.

"Let's get home." Francis pointed to Sabriel.

Lilly took the dagger and cut a hole for them to go home.

"Will it be different next time? The arena, where we train, I mean," Lilly questioned as they stepped back into the human world.

Cuff and Link, who had been waiting, ran towards them.

"Maybe a little. They will probably keep it the same for at least a little while though." He smiled at her excitement.

"Is Abditus... purgatory?" Lilly drew the fuller down the curtain between the worlds, sealing it.

"No, not at all. It's a plane between the worlds, where everything meets."

"Demons are there too, then?" Lilly asked as they began walking back to the cars.

"Not many; the angels can't patrol everywhere all the time, but the demons numbers are dwindling, they fear our power and numbers. They have for many years now. Now with you, there will be very few to worry about outside of Hell," Francis reassured her.

"No pressure," Lilly mumbled, leaning down to pet Cuff as they stopped at their cars.

"I'm beat. I can't wait for bed." As Lilly said it, she looked around at the sky, taking in the setting sun.

"Oh, but it's only--" Francis looked at his watch. "Not even 5:30 yet."

"But--I mean, we... We were there for hours."

"Time is different in Abditus," Francis shrugged. "So there's plenty of time for all that homework."

Lilly bit the inside of her cheek and stared through narrow eyes. Francis had heard her thoughts that all the training meant she had no time for homework.

"Don't look so grim." He laughed before driving off.

CHAPTER 21

"A gentleman accepts the responsibility of his actions and bears the burden of their consequences."

William Faulkner

"He can't influence her, Gahd," said a short kid with a long, but well kept beard. He looked older, but only because of the facial hair. "I tried myself and nothing."

They were in a dim room furnished with only two chairs and a desk. Gahd sat in the chair behind the desk. Music pulsed in the background; there was some form of a nightclub on the other side of the walls, but there was no door into the room. The only way in was to Fade through Abditus.

"This may be harder than we thought, Samael." Gahd drifted into thought.

"Don't you think I should just take over then? I will accomplish much more in less time."

"No. It has to be him," she hissed. "And Sybil? What has she revealed?"

"Just crazy undecipherable chatter. Nothing important. And Seymour is off the radar now."

Gahd took a sharp breath. "He's coming. Go home, and don't come back until I call you. Tell me when Sybil speaks."

Sam Faded. No sooner was he gone than Zeke was there.

"Finally."

"Look, Gahd--" Zeke started.

"I don't like your tone."

"This isn't for me, Gahd, I can't do this." Zeke paced.

"If you're backing out, thinking of running, you know we will find you." She circled him. "We will always find you."

"There has to be another way." Zeke stepped to her desperately. "What is it you want from her, just tell me-"

"I've told you your part!" She seemed to grow two feet as she hovered over him shouting.

Zeke sat back into a chair, feeling small and defeated.

"There's no other way and if you run, they," she looked up, "won't be the first to find you this time." She sat back down. "You have three weeks to damn her." Gahd leaned across her desk, eyes blazing. "Or I will drag you both to Hell myself."

Zeke snorted. "I'd like to see you try."

She opened her mouth to say more, but he disappeared.

CHAPTER 22

"False friends are like our shadow, keeping close to us while we walk in the sunshine, but leaving us when we cross into the shade."

Christian Nestell Bovee

Lilly rolled out of bed in a sweat from her latest dream. This time she saw John and tripped into a free fall off a cliff, landing in bed. Every time she fell back asleep she saw his face, or a demon's face, or Zeke.

There was a tap at her door. The clock read 5:00am. Lilly rubbed her eyes and threw on her running gear.

They agreed she would run Monday, Wednesday, Friday, and Saturday mornings. Wednesdays were self-defense. Tuesdays, Thursdays, Fridays, and Saturdays were Abditus training. Francis agreed to do extra training that Saturday so Lilly could hang out with her friends after school. Sundays and Mondays Francis would teach her, if she wanted, from his books, and about her mom.

This morning Francis ran ahead, allowing her to clear her mind and go more at her own pace. Or as much at her own pace as Cuff and Link would allow. When she returned with two happy tail-wagging dogs, Francis wished her luck at school that day and was off. Lilly wondered what he did with his days and where his money came from. Did he work or was there some sort of secret reserve for Jumper angels?

Lilly ran through the possibilities all day at school, her mind never crossing her schoolwork. She thought of going back to Abditus, and her invisible dagger, Sabriel, strapped to her belt. She wondered when she might have to use it. During lunch she thought she saw Zeke's eyes wander to Sabriel, or was she imagining things?

She kept an eye out all day for who might be more than just human, who else might be a Half Life, demon, or manipulator in training. But no one drew any attention except for Thaddeus and Zeke. She was convinced Thaddeus was a Manipulator since he didn't have wings, but his eyes glowed green and he had an energy about him she couldn't pinpoint, his aura she assumed. Ms. Lyons had eluded her all day, but Lilly was determined to find her soon and expose what she was.

With the weekend nearly here, most of Lilly's classmates were too focused on the last bell of the day to worry about what had happened earlier in the week. Even so, Elaine and Derek still found time to scowl at her, but for the most part Lilly's time in the limelight was over.

That was the funny thing. What happened to John would pass for his classmates, but for John there was a long challenging road ahead of him. Who knew where he would be sent, maybe a juvenile detention center? He might keep in touch with a few friends if his parents let him, but he would never return to Wakefield High. His peers had no clue the journey ahead of him, that his life was changed forever.

And they had no idea what lay ahead for Lilly. No one knew she had been given a task by the Archangels to fight a war against pure evil. They had no idea that Lilly would spend most of her free time training not for a marathon, but to kill demons. John and Lilly were not all too different.

"Where to first?" Erica raised her eyebrows as she and Dawn opened the doors to her Volkswagen bug.

"Anywhere, let's just go." Jen rushed by, bumping into Lilly, nearly knocking her over.

Lilly opened her mouth to shout at Jen, but Kathy silently motioned for Lilly not to say anything.

"Leave your cars here--I'll drive." Kathy pointed to her SUV.

Piling into Kathy's SUV, Erica and Dawn broke the silence with ideas for the Friday evening ahead of them.

As Quinn and Amir drove past, Quinn smiled at Lilly. When Lilly tried to smile back she got too nervous and looked away. She looked back at him to see if he even caught her smile, but he was already gone. What she did see was Jen's boyfriend, Andy.

Suddenly, everything held still. Andy's eyes were pure red and a black shadow consumed him, a black shadow Lilly knew no one else could see. She held her arms down, trying not to dawn attention as her wrists blazed with pain.

"Let's go," Lilly uttered to Kathy.

"Where?"

"The mall?" Dawn offered.

"Yeah, let's go," Lilly said.

Jen caught Andy's look of rage and locked her door. "Kathy…"

The others looked up to see where Lilly's and Jen's eyes were set. "JEN!" Andy roared, marching towards them, his hands in fists.

"Well sh…." Kathy muttered as she threw the car in reverse and tore out of the parking spot.

Andy stood in the middle of the road watching as they drove off.

"What the hell was that?" Kathy glared at Jen in the rear view, but Jen stared out the window, silent.

"Jen." Erica nudged her.

"He's just being a jerk," Jen blurted out.

"About…?"

"Andy wanted to hang out."

"He's stalking you because we're having a girls' night?" Kathy sped up; her voice was raging.

"Yeah..." her voice was faint.

They all fell silent. Jen's phone buzzed a few times and she took it out to answer.

"Don't you dare! Turn it off." Kathy looked to Erica.

Erica snatched the phone and turned it off. Jen opened her mouth to argue, but thought better of it.

Lilly was finally beginning to calm down. The pains in her wrists had made her angry this time to the point she had to keep herself from getting out of the car. She didn't know what she wanted to do to Andy, she just knew she didn't want to wait in the car for him to get to them.

Erica and Dawn chatted away as Kathy drove them to the mall, but the others stayed quiet. Lilly wondered if her friends would believe that she knew Andy was possessed.

"I just moved in so it's a bit of a mess." Lilly fumbled with her apartment keys.

They had walked every corridor of the mall, checking out their favorite clothing stores and saying hi to the others' friends. On their way back, everyone had picked up their cars from school and followed Lilly home.

"Yeah, yeah," Jen rolled her eyes.

"We don't care," Dawn chimed in.

"As long as there's no adults," Erica shrugged.

"We don't have a lot of furniture yet."

The girls laughed as Dawn mimicked her behind her back, making Lilly wonder what was funny about not having furniture.

At top of the steps, Francis's door creaked open. As usual, he was in his running gear with the dogs.

"Oh, Lilly!" His muscles were very evident through his thin tight shirt and his smile radiated to each of the girls, except Lilly, who scowled at him. She knew well enough that he was purposefully leaving at the exact moment they arrived.

"Really Lilly, it's fine," Kathy beamed at Francis.

Lilly turned to look at Kathy and noticed the words float above her head, *Andy doesn't know where you live...'* At first Lilly was startled at the sight. She wondered why this was the first time she had noticed it happen today.

She wanted you to know, that's why. Francis's voice was in her head.

"Francis," Lilly's stare turned to Francis.

"Thanks again for helping out with the dogs this week."

Cuff and Link wagged their little butts over and licked their hands.

"Anytime," Lilly smiled. "This is, uh, Erica and Dawn... you know Jen, and Kathy."

"Nice to meet you, ladies. I'll see you at self-defense next Wednesday?"

"Yes!" Jen nearly burst out of her skin.

The others nodded uncontrollably.

"Enjoy your night, ladies." He winked at Lilly as he made his way down the steps, whistling the whole way.

Lilly tried her best to wait until her back was turned to roll her eyes. She reminded herself how lonely Francis must be and took a deep breath. As soon as the outside door shut they all gushed over how cute Francis is, except Lilly.

"Did you see his chest?"

"Hottest neighbor ever!"

"He is soooo crushing on you Lilly!"

"Ew, no." Lilly's face contorted as she unlocked her door and walked in.

"Are you seriously saying you don't dig him?"

"He's too old, I would never consider it." Lilly put her backpack down on the dining room table. She paused. *Since when did I have a dining room table?* Looking around, the entire apartment was fully furnished and decorated with paintings, vases, and fresh flowers. Lilly stood dumbfounded.

"He's gotta be like in college."

"Late college."

"More like Doctorate..."

"Yeah, totally illegal, like thirty."

"Whatever, he's still hot."

"I mean we graduate in six months, we're not kids anymore."

"He's a pain," Lilly grumbled and they laughed.

"You totally dig him," Kathy said.

Erica started looking through Lilly's bookshelf, or rather Francis's bookshelf, with a few of her own books, but mostly books Lilly had never seen before. Lilly tried her best not to look startled at all the new things in her home, as they settled in. Erica stopped at the bottom shelf.

"Wakefield High 1996. For real? Ha!" She plopped down on a brand new L-shaped leather sofa with the yearbook.

"Drinks?" Jen emerged from the kitchen with five glasses. She sat them on the coffee table and took a bottle from her backpack.

Dawn grabbed a glass and took a sip. "You have any snacks?"

"Uh, yeah..." Lilly cringed when she turned away from them, not sure what she could really offer them, maybe one frozen pizza.

"You guys gotta check this out," Erica stared at the yearbook.

Kathy sat down next to her, drink in hand. "Lilly."

"Just a minute..." Lilly sighed as she opened the fridge.

To her surprise it was filled with drinks, salsa, fruit, veggies, burgers. She opened the freezer and there were more pizzas, chicken nuggets, and other snacks she was sure Francis didn't actually approve of. Sliding her phone from her pocket, she preheated the oven.

'WHAT THE HECK FRANCIS, STOP GIVING ME THINGS!' She texted Francis. She threw the pizza in the oven and went to sit down with the others.

"Is this your parents'?" Kathy asked.

"My mom, I'm not sure where my dad went." Lilly leaned in.

"Check out the shorts on the basketball team," Erica giggled.

Jen was flipping through TV stations ignoring them, only taking the time to pour herself another glass.

"Wait, go back, go back," Kathy uttered.

"What?"

She flipped the page and pointed. "Look!"

"Is that?"

"What the?"

"That looks just like Zeke," Lilly said.

"Nah, his nose is completely different," Jen chimed in after barely glancing at the page.

"It's probably his dad," Dawn said.

"Your parents must have known each other," Kathy smiled, then sat back to watch the TV.

Lilly sat back herself and considered the thought. Was it actually Zeke? Her phone buzzed.

'YOU'RE WELCOME FOR SPENDING ALL DAY MAKING YOUR PLACE LOOK COOL, CABLE AND INTERNET ON ME :-P"

Lilly made a face at her phone.

'THANK YOU FRANCIS... HOW LONG DOES A HALF LIFE LIVE? DO THEY AGE?'

"Bathroom?" Jen stood up.

"Down the hall to the left." Lilly pointed.

"Oh, The Parent Trap!" Dawn snagged the remote from Kathy.

Erica groaned.

"What? How could you not love this? Finding your long lost sister!"

"We should invite boys over." Erica stared at her fingernails, after making a face at Dawn.

Kathy leaned on Dawn's shoulder and yawned. "Lilly?"

"Sure…" Lilly took out her phone to see Francis's reply.

'UNTIL THEY DECIDE WHERE THEY BELONG, NOT REALLY.'

Erica peeked at her phone, "Are you texting Francis?" Erica's voice was filled with excitement.

"Uh… Yeah…" Lilly grinned awkwardly and slid her phone away before Erica saw what they were texting about.

"Ooo la la, Lilly!" Kathy nudged her.

The toilet flushed and Jen exited the bathroom. She pushed the door open to Lilly's bedroom. "This is a one bedroom apartment," Jen's voice rang accusingly through the apartment. She strutted down the hall directly to Lilly. "Is this even your place? Where are all your family photos?"

Unable to think, Lilly's mouth hung open and her face turned bright red.

"Cool it, Jen," Kathy snapped.

"You live alone?" Dawn asked.

"That's awesome!"

"I, my parents," Lilly stood up, "they travel a lot and prefer me to stay here, with closer neighbors." She brushed past Jen into the kitchen. Lying was becoming easier and easier for her, and more fun.

"We have a lot of land in Pennsylvania. It's just better for me to be here while they're gone, rather than live alone on a boring farm by myself." Lilly pulled the pizza from the oven, the aroma catching their attention. "You know, until school's out."

"I'm starving!" Kathy got up to help Lilly in the kitchen.

"Bring me a slice."

"Me too."

Jen scoffed and sat down, texting on her phone.

"Ignore her," Kathy whispered.

Lilly leaned back on the counter and shrugged. She texted Francis, 'SO ZEKE KNEW MY MOM THEN.'

"You know, misery loves company." Kathy had gotten out plates and started slicing the pizza. "We might need another pizza."

"Especially if Erica invites boys," Lilly replied.

"You can tell her no, Lilly. It's ok."

"I don't mind." She paused. "Hey, do you have Zeke's number?"

"Yeaaaah," Kathy grinned. "Should we invite him?"

"Text it to me."

Francis had taken Cuff and Link for a short run before returning to his apartment. He took off their collars and hung them next to the door, then left his running shoes on the mat next to the door. He hung up his keys and his jacket, slid on his slippers, and heated up a pre-made meal from the refrigerator.

When Francis had first become human he enjoyed eating. The tastes were unlike anything he had before as an angel. But over the years it had become more of a hassle having to fuel his body with precisely what it needed, staying healthy and well balanced.

Every Sunday he took time to prepare his meals for the week, so he wouldn't have to bother cooking much during the week. It wasn't that he didn't have time. Francis had plenty of time to do anything he wanted. He just had a certain distaste for the repetitive tasks like preparing meals, doing laundry, dishes.

Exercise was one of the few repetitive things that he truly enjoyed. The burning of his muscles and the speeds he reached when running made him feel happy, alive. He found it interesting the way his body changed, his muscles got bigger or more defined when he worked out more.

As an angel he was whatever he wanted to be with no physical work, a reflection of how he perceived himself, but here he enjoyed the work behind how he looked. He read something about endorphins being released when someone works out, making them happy. Francis considered the science behind what he already knew about the human body.

Cuff and Link cuddled up on the sofa waiting for Francis, who picked out his favorite book from the shelf. It was thick like a textbook. Its dull brown spine read, 'World Science' to discourage anyone from taking it off the shelf and cracking open its pages. But inside it was a handwritten book written by Francis and a few others who aided in the training of every single past Keeper of the sword. It was Francis's guide to teaching Lilly everything she needed to know, everything to guide her and keep the world safe.

Francis took the time to read over it as often as possible to remind himself of when things went wrong in the past, the best ways to teach about different demons, or when the best time to have a Keeper kill for the first time was. Tonight, Francis wanted to read something Gabriel had written a few hundred years ago about a Keeper and Nightmares.

He had just gotten settled into the book when there was a commotion in the hallway. Cuff and Link raised their heads, releasing low growls. Peeking at his phone, Francis found a text from Lilly from thirty minutes ago.

"Zeke…" Francis grumbled.

He crept to the door and peered out the peephole. Four guys, including Zeke, stood outside Lilly's door. Erica opened the door, welcoming them in her bubbliest of voices. Before the door closed Zeke looked back and grinned at Francis. Francis's hands curled into fists. The dogs were at his side. Too smart to bark, they just grumbled quietly at the door.

Without a second thought, Francis flung the door open and marched towards Lilly's door. But before he got to the door, Chamuel appeared in front of him, blocking his path. Everything seemed to slow when she appeared: the voices inside Lilly's apartment, the hum of someone's clothes dryer, even the music coming from a neighbor's apartment slowed to half speed.

Chamuel's red hair covered half her face; the half he could see was irritated. One hand held her staff and the other sat on the hilt of her sword in its sheath. She stared down at him, taking in his distress.

As an angel she would be almost twice the size as any human, but she chose to appear to Francis only slightly taller than him, probably because the hallway only permitted her to be a certain height. Her wings were displayed just slightly, to make herself look larger. Taking her hand off her sword, Chamuel reached into a small pouch hanging from her belt and pulled out a handful of shimmering dust.

"Go." Chamuel held her hand out flat and blew the strange dusty substance onto the dogs, who began to whimper. Both Cuff and Link turned and ran back into their apartment, straight *through* the wall into their apartment. Chamuel smiled. "You too." She waved her hand dismissively. "I'd rather not... dust you." Her voice was cocky and content.

"Let's see how that would work for you," he snapped. "Now leave me to this, Chamuel."

"You're not to help, that's straight from the mouth of Michael."

"Zeke is meant to kill her, Cha. Thaddeus heard from a Manipulator that is close to Skoal, Zeke's mentor."

"We know. Her Guardians will protect her if it comes to that."

Francis acted as if he didn't hear her and tried to power past her. It was no use though, she hardly had to place her hand on his shoulder and no sooner did he stumble back a few feet. His eyes narrowed and he stood prepared to challenge her.

"You grow weak in your human form, old friend."

Ignoring her, he said, "I won't watch her die."

"Save your strength, no one dies tonight."

"I still have a few tricks." He stepped forward. "Things you, things Michael, don't even know."

"Four angels to one Half Life, Francis. We have it covered. Zeke is nothing. Now go." She raised her hand and an unseen force pushed him back.

The guys had brought more drinks and were more than happy to share. Lilly was getting chips and salsa when Zeke followed her into the kitchen.

"So, Jen tells me you live here alone." He raised his eyebrows.

Lilly stopped pouring the salsa into a bowl and turned to him. "Don't play games with me, Zeke. You knew my mom. I saw her yearbook. You know more than you're letting on."

Zeke's lip curled up into an uneasy smile. "Smart girl."

"Then tell me... everything."

"Not here. I can do one better though, I can *show you*."

"What?" Lilly picked up the bowl of salsa.

"I can take you to an oracle." He reached out and touched her arm, causing pains to shoot through her wrists. She let out a high-pitched cry and dropped the bowl. They watched as it shattered on the tile floor.

Zeke jumped back, surprised at her reaction to his touch.

"Everything OK in here?" Kathy peeked in grinning.

Kathy and Erica were making kissy faces behind Zeke's back. They seemed to think her cry was a pleasant one.

"Yeah, fine, just dropped the salsa."

Kathy winked and left them alone again, but she had to pull Erica away.

Zeke hadn't taken his eyes off Lilly, watching as her left hand reached down to Sabriel on her belt. Its hilt shimmered blue. He glanced up at her, but really it was like he was looking beyond her. He took a few steps back, shaking his head.

"I'm sorry, Lilly, I'm sorry." Zeke's voice was filled with terror. He backed away until he was out of sight, leaving Lilly to clean up the mess.

"What was all that about?" Kathy stepped into the kitchen after the front door slammed shut. "He didn't even say bye."

"I'm not sure…" Lilly bent down to clean up the salsa.

CHAPTER 23

"Life is really simple, but we insist on making it complicated."
Confucius

"Gahd, she has Sabriel," Zeke shouted into the phone.

"Yes, I'm sure of it!" Skoal stood at Zeke's side, worried.

"So? You have decades of experience, she has not even a month," Gahd hissed.

"Four Guardians, I saw them when I told her about the oracle! Who has four guardian angels, Gahd? And Sabriel! Where am I even supposed to get an oracle from anyway? Sybil is missing!" He stood, livid. "What have you gotten me into? This is a suicide mission. Any way I look at it, I lose!"

"I'm confident you'll find a way," she said lazily. "If not, you'll be my pet for eternity," she added before hanging up.

"Gahd doesn't know that you know Lilly is the Keeper?" Skoal asked.

Zeke dropped his face into his palms and shook his head.

"Good. Call Samael."

"He isn't answering; his house is vacant."

Skoal tapped the table with his fingertips. "Seymour is in hiding. Maybe Thaddeus..." Skoal Faded.

CHAPTER 24

"If you can't fly then run, if you can't run then walk, if you can't walk then crawl, but whatever you do you have to keep moving forward."

Martin Luther King, Jr.

"I'm up, I'm up," Lilly yawned as she stumbled down the steps.

It was 5am on a Saturday and Lilly's friends were still sleeping, but Lilly had to run. Francis stayed behind and Lilly let Cuff and Link guide her. Really she had no choice, they were quite willing to drag her wherever they pleased.

After three miles, she was slightly less out of breath than her last run. Her friends were still sleeping in her apartment and despite her tiredness, Lilly could not sleep after running. So, she made breakfast. Scrambled eggs, bacon she didn't remember buying, and she sat some frozen waffles on the counter.

Lilly had placed her schedule on the refrigerator with a magnet from Adrian. She touched Francis's writing; today was Abditus, she smiled.

"You're such a good host."

Kathy stood in the hallway still in her clothes from the night before. Her hair was a mess and her make up was smeared and fading. *It's nice to see her smiling disheveled face in the morning,* Lilly thought. Dragging her feet, Kathy crossed the kitchen and gave Lilly a lazy side hug.

"I'm glad we're friends. …But I really need to pee." She shuffled off to the bathroom, leaving Lilly amused.

Slowly everyone woke up, one by one grabbing some breakfast and leaving. Erica and Dawn wanted to go back to the mall and get some clothes they had liked, but had talked themselves out of the day before. According to Kathy this was a routine thing and they would probably talk themselves out of it again today. Kathy had to get to work and Jen didn't really say anything, just a quick bye.

Before Lilly had a chance to sit down from cleaning up her messy apartment, there was a knock on the door. Francis was there waiting, ready to leave for Abditus.

"Let me change real quick--"

"Don't bother, Suriel is just going to change your outfit when we get there, anyway," Francis stated.

"What did you do last night?" Lilly asked, trying to spark conversation on their ride to the park at Oregon Ridge.

"Just relaxed."

"Nice." Lilly thought for a moment. "What are we doing today?"

Francis shrugged.

"Another obstacle course?"

"Yes."

Frustrated by his simple answers, Lilly rested her head back on the seat and closed her eyes. She imagined Zeke again, talking about the oracle, and dropping the salsa dish. It shattered. It shattered. Lilly jerked up right as the truck pulled to a stop.

"You OK?" Francis asked, his tone flat.

"Yeah."

They grabbed their bags and Lilly followed Francis into the woods silently. He picked a random spot and stopped.

Francis motioned to Sabriel.

The dagger was cold and heavy in Lilly's hand. She held it out straight at a gap between two trees.

"You're quiet today..." She dragged Sabriel through the air, cutting a nice tall opening.

The now loose curtain-like edge flapped in the cold morning air, moving the edge of the tree back and forth like an ocean wave. The waving tree drew her attention and she reached out to touch it. There was a small carving on the trunk, a ' Þ ', like the rune, she thought.

"Just tired, didn't sleep much last night." Francis pushed through the opening, distracting her from the symbol.

When she turned from sealing the hole, Lilly found they were actually standing *in* the arena. There were already a few angels gathered, but not nearly as many as before. Chamuel, Suriel, and Raziel were there, but Gabriel and Jophiel were missing, along with the elusive Michael and Raphael.

The agility course was completely different today with a rock climbing wall, rope climb, and a mud pit with electrical wire above it to crawl under. Then there was a path of short balance beams and thin posts she had to walk on and jump to and from each one without falling to the ground. Raziel eagerly added a fire illusion under the beams and posts, or at least she hoped it was an illusion. If she fell or got stuck, she had to start over.

Lilly's favorite part was at the top of the rope climb, where it ended at a platform. She was twenty feet up and had to swing on a rope cross a giant lake to the finish line, a platform. She was amazed the lake could exist in the void of Abditus.

But Lilly was so hot the first time she ran through the course that she decided to drop down halfway through the swing right into the cool lake. Raziel and Suriel laughed and clapped along with some of the other angels that had gathered. But Francis and Chamuel were not amused. She ended up back at the top of the swing each time she dropped into the lake; she assumed it was Chamuel's doing.

"What does this have to do with finding the sword and killing demons?" Lilly panted as she finished a two-mile run around the coliseum.

"Have you ever fought a demon?" Chamuel's eyes glared down at her.

"Well, no, but--"

"I have killed thousands of demons. I can't imagine how exhausting it would be to do as a human. Your bodies are so fragile and weak compared to ours. All we can do is *try* to toughen you up, so you might not die so soon," she sneered.

"Chamuel!" Raziel's voice thundered.

But Chamuel didn't show the slightest hint of regret; really she seemed quite satisfied with Lilly's frightened expression. Chamuel flapped her wings once and she was gone.

"Chamuel is no help with weaponry anyway. She always uses blunt force," Suriel said, matter of fact.

Raziel snapped his fingers and the room filled with every weapon imaginable, except guns. Lilly followed Raziel and Suriel into the room.

Francis had disappeared after her run.

"It's so… I really don't want to fight…" She wrinkled her nose.

"We're only preparing you for the worst." Suriel placed her hand on Lilly's shoulder.

"But the worst, it will come, won't it?"

Suriel half smiled at her and handed Lilly a mace. It had a long wooden handle with a chain attached to a big spiked sphere. If she hadn't had such a good grip on it she would have dropped it altogether; instead it fell to the ground with Lilly still holding tight to the handle. Suriel made it look so light.

They introduced her to over a dozen types of weapons: swords, throwing stars, daggers, a disk weapon meant to decapitate its assailant, and many more.

"It's all in the wrist," Raziel cooed as he chucked a throwing star at a target. It hit dead center. He motioned for Lilly to try next.

"All in the wrist…" Lilly made a few practice motions before snapping her wrist and letting go. She over-threw and the star went flying at the nearest column, made contact, and then came flying back straight at Lilly. It lodged in her right arm.

Raziel and Suriel looked at each other, baffled. Lilly looked at her arm, then to her angel companions, then back to her arm, as her chest heaved in panic.

"Well, you don't throw very hard," Raziel broke the silence and pulled the star out of Lilly's arm, blood gushing out. "If a demon was next to you and you got it a foot over, that would have been some trick." Suriel placed her hand over Lilly's arm. When she took it away, Lilly's arm was healed, just blood on her shirt remained.

By the end of the session Lilly had managed to mangle herself with three different weapons. The star, the disk, and the mace all made their mark on her.

"Well, you could use some practice." Raziel shrugged.

"On anything thrown," Suriel tried to smile.

"Or swung," Lilly said.

The angels laughed and nudged her thoughtfully.

"The mace was definitely the most painful," Lilly uttered, making them laugh again.

They sat down in front of the magical dry erase board again. Lilly was sweaty and out of breath from their lesson, but Raziel and Suriel never broke their comfortable nature.

Francis was waiting for them in the classroom when they entered, looking perturbed.

"Hey, the mace takes balance, and a lot of practice."

"Don't get used to the pain," Raziel shook his head.

Lilly looked down at her notebook a little embarrassed.

Diligently, Lilly wrote down every word that came from Raziel and Suriel. She barely looked up from her notebook. They taught first about Succubi, female demons who seduce people and then steal their souls in the process.

Next was Jiin, demons that could change into any human or animal form and then slowly feed off their human counterpart until they are too weak to fight for their souls. Suriel explained Jinn are commonly sent to take the souls of the stronger willed as they can go undetected for so long. By the time the human realizes something is wrong, it's too late.

"The easiest way for you to identify a demon is by their eyes or the faint form you will notice from the sight that Iris gave you. The weaker demons will be very visible to you—their eyes glow red, sometimes green, or just black or yellow depending on their rank. You may see remnants of Hell on them--firey, scaly, dry, wrinkly or decaying skin, animal-like features, bat-like wings. Though, some still have wings like ours," Suriel said.

"During the day light," Raziel continued, "most demons are able to hide their true form, at least to those who don't have the sight. They will look like any other human being. But in the moonlight all demons true forms are shown."

"At night they will be completely cloaked to hide themselves, or indoors."

"They can hide in the dark, but not in the light of the dark," Lilly added.

"Right!" Suriel smiled. "You were born to do this."

Lilly half smiled. "What about the demon that chased me after school that day? It looked like a demon in daylight. Why?"

"A lowly Nit demon, a newborn, they can barely control their actions, let alone their appearance. It was only sent to scare you," Francis said frankly.

This was the most Francis had said to her all day.

She glanced at Francis's stiff face; he didn't return a look to Lilly. She turned back to her work and jotted down a few words, waiting for Raziel and Suriel to continue. Suriel exchanged a look with Raziel.

"Once you identify the type of demon you will then know how to send them back to Hell. Jinn and Succubi have the same weakness."

Raziel explained that demons are vain and can easily be slowed down by a mirror or some sort of reflection. Then they can be destroyed or captured in them.

"Mirrors work well on Jinn and Succubi in particular. Then once distracted, their heads must be chopped off to prevent them from changing form or tempting you," Suriel said.

Unable to control herself, Lilly shuddered.

"Thus why we don't use guns, bullets scarcely slow down most demons. Only losing their head or large wounds, or special weapons like the Ferryman, kill them," Raziel added.

"I was wondering…" Lilly said.

Continuing with sword technique, they went back to the armory to visually go over it with Lilly.

"When you find the Ferryman, you must take a knee and claim it," Suriel told her.

"Yes, that's the first thing you do, you say 'with the power of this sword I take authority as the new Keeper.' Repeat it." Francis nodded.

"With the power of this sword I take authority as the new Keeper."

"Good, repeat it every day."

"Here." Suriel handed her a sword to practice with.

With each slash of a sword and toss of a throwing star, Lilly worked on pushing the thought of what these objects would really do one day out of her mind. She reminded herself that a demon was evil, and the angels here, that taught her, were good. Everyone knew that. And killing a demon was OK, they were bad. She pictured her mom killing a demon.

"What's an oracle?" Lilly blurted out as she sat down an ancient haladie. The image of Zeke grabbing her and Lilly dropping the salsa popped into her mind. She looked up and the image floated above her.

Her face burned bright red. Raziel and Suriel both took a step back, watching as Francis shuddered with anger.

"What does 'stay away from Zeke' mean to you?" He roared. Lilly shook her head, backing away from him. "He *will* get you killed, Lilly!"

There was nowhere else for Lilly to back up; she was against a table filled with weapons and Francis's face just inches from hers.

"I'm sorry… I'm sorry…" she whispered, but then her face turned cross. She stood up straight and leaned into him. "I'm still learning, Francis. You tell me how to fight and what to do, but not why. Not what happened to my mom or why Zeke is so dangerous. Just an, 'I'll tell you later' to every important question. And you expect me to just sit back and do as you say? All of you!" Her voice was angry, but level. She had been ready to tell Francis and the others off about this crazy trust fall they expected of her since she got beat up after school.

"You--" Francis started.

Suriel slid herself between them. "It's been a long week, loves." She put her arm around Francis and redirected him.

"How about a direct flight home?" Raziel held his hand out to Lilly.

"Gladly." She took his hand.

Raziel's wings spread to full span.

"Michael," Suriel uttered to Francis and the pair disappeared as Suriel touched his arm.

Without warning Raziel took Lilly around the midsection with one arm and pulled her to his side. "Hold tight!" His deep voice shook her. Flapping his wings once, the air around them moved so fast Lilly had to close her eyes. When it stopped she opened them to find herself back in her apartment. "Nice place."

"Thanks Raz," Lilly said. "I left my backpack…"

"On it!" One second Raziel was gone, the next he returned to her side, dropping her backpack next to her. "Don't mind Francis, he's only human. You're doing wonderful, my dear." Raziel bowed before disappearing again.

CHAPTER 25

"Never to suffer would never to have been blessed."
Edgar Allan Poe

Lilly spent the next twenty-four hours avoiding Francis. She stayed home, attempting to finish her homework, but Kathy invited her out Saturday night, so she gladly went bowling. Erica and Jen joined them along with Quinn and Amir, and some of the guys from the night before, except Zeke. Lilly wondered if Francis had warned Zeke to stay away, but quickly shook the thought off, wanting to get back to enjoying her new friends.

The friends who thought she was fun and cool because she was the new kid who lived alone. The friends who had no idea she was a supposed future demon killer with no mom.

"Hey Lil" Vincent's voice echoed through her phone Sunday morning.

"Vincent."

"I know you're not happy to hear from me, I just wanted to see how you're doing."

"Honestly," Lilly took a deep breath, "I'm doing great, I finally feel like I'm where I belong."

"That's really great to hear. Really, I'm happy you're happy." They fell silent. "I'm going home for Thanksgiving, maybe you can make the trip too? It wouldn't be the same without you."

Lilly reminded herself of all the holidays she spent at home without Vincent. "I've made a lot of friend here Vin, and already made plans for Thanksgiving, that whole weekend actually," she lied. "But tell Dad and Emma I say hi." Lilly paused. "And I miss them."

"OK."

"I have a lot of homework."

"Yeah, me too," Vincent said honestly.

"Thanks for calling."

"Love ya, Lil."

"You too."

Other than Vincent, no one called her or bothered her all day Sunday. She tried not to think about her dad or Emma, even though she really should return their calls. She had gotten through all her homework early and by mid-afternoon had no idea what to do with herself. Having read through most of one of her favorite books, Fahrenheit 451, she made an origami butterfly, and was working on a triceratops when there was a knock on the door.

The peephole revealed it was Francis. Lilly smiled and then her face contorted, remembering she had been angry with him. She leaned against the door to take a deep breath. She was battling her feelings of anger mixed with how happy it made her to see him.

"Lilly."

She opened the door.

He looked a bit out of sorts; his shirt was wrinkled and he looked like he hadn't slept in days. "I'm sorry, Lilly."

"It's OK, Francis…" she looked down and tapped her fingers against her hip. "I was getting bored without you telling me what to do," she chuckled.

A smile perked from one side of his mouth. "I uh, just made dinner if you'd like to…"

"Yes."

"Oh, well, great, I have something to show you."

Francis's living room was scattered with open boxes and their contents were spilling out of them. One was filled with women's clothes that mainly looked like workout gear in every color, but mostly purple and red. Another was filled with pictures of her mom with friends, Lilly assumed, since she didn't recognize them as family, and some personal belongings.

"Eva--your mom's things. I got them out of storage yesterday."

"She traveled a lot," Lilly noted.

"You will, too."

"Why do you have all this and not my dad?"

Francis shrugged. "You can have it now."

Lilly took out a photo of Francis and Eva at the beach and placed it on the coffee table. "Were you together?"

"No, no never. It was never like that. I jumped, I came here to help take care of you kids," Francis said immediately.

Lilly took out another photo with Francis and a very young Vincent. "I don't remember you much."

"All your memories didn't come back?"

Lilly shook her head. "I always assumed I blocked out my childhood, before you gave me memories."

"That may be true."

Lilly dug through the boxes. "Yeah..."

The pair talked about Eva and the years before Lilly was born. Every memory Francis had to offer was a gem to Lilly.

Francis had prepared homemade lasagna for dinner. They ate while watching what Francis said was Eva's favorite movie, The Mummy. About half way through Lilly's eyelids gave in.

"Lilly," Francis whispered, his arm stuck under Lilly's resting head, but Lilly was already asleep. He carefully lifted her and laid her down on the sofa. He placed a blanket over her and let the movie run. He was ready for bed himself. He clicked for the dogs, but when they didn't follow him he turned to see they had already curled up with Lilly.

"Traitors," He muttered jokingly.

Mummies flooded her dreams. They chased her until she fell off a rickety bridge. Again and again, she dreamt the same thing until his voice finally woke her.

"Lilly." Francis nudged her.

When she opened her eyes, Francis held a finger over his mouth, trying to keep her calm and quiet. "Sabriel." He pointed to the dagger on the coffee table next to her. She reached for it, feeling the heavy breathing behind her head. Her hand rested on top of Sabriel as she turned to see the gruesome stumpy gargoyle creature lying on the sofa behind her head.

She whipped her head back around to Francis. "Nightmare?" She mouthed.

He nodded, pointing to the dagger again, and then making a jabbing motion. Francis stepped back a few feet to where the dogs lay; he had told them to stay before he woke her.

Slowly she moved out from under the blanket, trying not to disturb the resting creature. But those things were light sleepers once their prey was awake. It rustled on her pillows.

She tried to breathe easy and even as she got a good look at it. Its skin looked much like an alligator's--a short stumpy alligator with a wrinkly round face and big ears.

"Settle." Francis put his hand on her back.

"I have to kill it," Lilly said, unsure.

Again she took a deep breath as she closed her eyes and loosened her knees. When her eyes opened the creature was at the edge of the sofa growling and ready to attack her.

"How did it get past your spells?"

"It's been attached to you since you moved here."

Lilly looked horrified. "And you never told me?" She said accusingly, but the creature snapped at her hand, drawing her attention away from Francis.

"Concentrate," Francis said.

She held the dagger to the side like Jophiel had taught her, ready to strike. It began glowing blue and the glow extended around her hand. Francis stepped back. Thrashing the knife out at the beast, Lilly swiped Sabriel to the side and sliced the nightmare's shoulder. It screeched, revealing four sets of tiny teeth on top *and* bottom. She knew she was supposed to punch, but at the last second she used the knife, out of fear.

Before Francis had a chance to correct her, the creature jumped at Lilly and latched onto her right forearm. Sabriel dropped from her grasp. Lilly didn't panic, knowing Francis was there if she needed him, so she waved him back.

The pain ebbed down through her hand and shot straight up her arm. She grabbed the creature by its throat with her left hand. It released her right arm and Lilly threw it into the wall.

Its head smacked the wall with a thud and it rolled around on its back before jumping to attention. It snapped and snarled at Francis and Lilly.

"C'mon," she beckoned the creature. Her right arm lay limp at her side, but Lilly had snatched Sabriel up again in her left hand and it was glowing blue, ready to go.

After circling each other, the creature leaped, a lot more agile than one might expect, right at Lilly's throat. Before it had a chance to bite, she punched it straight between the eyes with Sabriel so hard it soared through the air. The blue glow started to envelop it and the creature screamed horribly. The blue glow completely consumed the Nightmare, and it vanished.

Lilly leaned against the wall, taking a look at her bloody, crippled arm. "Well that sucks." She blacked out.

———————

When she came to she was on Francis's sofa with Cuff and Link licking her face.

"Get outta here, boys." He swatted them away. "Good job, Zenobia."

"Wah?" Lilly squinted, and then winced at the pain shooting through her arm.

"You probably would have lost your arm from the venom, but thankfully you have *thee* best angel healer in this universe here to help." His voice was stern as he mended her arm with a surgical suture.

Lilly just groaned before passing out again.

When she came to again her arm was mended and wrapped in clean bandages. She felt warm and sweaty as she tossed around. The pain was still unbearable and she knew she would pass out soon, or at least she hoped she would. Her eyes searched for Francis. He was sitting in the chair next to the sofa reading from an old science book.

At the sight of her movement he stood. "Hey, how do you feel?"

"Horrible. I'm missing school." Her eyelids grew heavy.

"Yes, tomorrow too, most likely."

"But... Ugh, I need pain meds," Lilly moaned.

Before she had a chance to say more, Francis's hand touched her forehead and she was instantly out.

The two days to follow were a blur. She had times where she was awake enough to send texts to her friends, who wanted to know where she was. Kathy had been so pushy she showed up. Francis made up a story that they had been hiking Sunday and a coyote attacked her. Lilly was awake enough to confirm the story, so Kathy seemed less skeptical and left after an hour visit.

By Wednesday she was able to go back to school and start training again. Despite the pain it caused to kill it, Lilly was glad the Nightmare was gone and she could sleep peacefully, without bad dreams.

"It would have taken even less time with less scarring if I had the proper medicines," Francis's perturbed voice echoed when she left for school Wednesday. He had bandaged her arm out of precaution, even though it was nearly healed.

For the next two weeks, Lilly trained as if there was a demon-hunting marathon approaching, and she had so much homework she would have forgotten all about her arm if it hadn't been for the few teeth marks the creature had left behind.

No one had seen Zeke in school since the night he rushed out of Lilly's apartment apologizing. *Good riddance,*

Lilly thought. He had caused so much turmoil between her and Francis.

She did still hope to meet the oracle for insight Francis didn't have on her mother. After looking it up, she found an oracle was basically a prophet. Lilly ascertained it could tell her the future or the past, but she didn't dare ask Francis more.

Each day her body was sorer than the last with training almost every single day.

"Drink this." Francis handed her a thick brown drink in a shaker one morning.

"What is this, *angel drugs*?" She joked.

"No," Francis snapped. "It's a protein and vitamin drink to help your body recover faster."

It flustered Francis so much Lilly called the drink 'angel drugs' every chance she got. Most days it won her an extra lap around the coliseum or a round of hurdles, which weren't so bad anymore. Once he had made her do weight training as punishment, but quickly realized Lilly enjoyed it too much for it to be punishment.

Jophiel had begun giving her lessons on Lito.

"I don't think you're teaching me properly on purpose!" Lilly burst out one day as her thoughts of Quinn walking her to class that day floated through the air.

Gabriel and Suriel laughed, still getting a kick out of her silly thoughts escaping her in Abditus.

"You're not learning properly," Jophiel retorted as he stared into the distance, uncaringly.

Every day she learned about a new demon. Francis had given her a book one Sunday that resembled a children's book. It was illustrated and the writing was simple to confuse any reader who picked it up into thinking it was *just a kids' book*. But it was not just a kids' book; it was a real book of secrets to the underworld.

She still had yet to meet Michael or Raphael, but the other Archangels often spoke of them. *Michael would want you to learn this,* or *Raphael once took out five legions of demons on his own.*

"Uh-huh," Lilly would reply blandly. *They probably don't exist,* Lilly thought and the words escaped her mind.

"They exist." Chamuel's eyes narrowed, staring her down in annoyance.

The Wednesday before Thanksgiving, everyone at Lilly's lunch table was talking about what they were doing with their families over the break. Lilly couldn't help but feel isolated.

"What are you doing for Thanksgiving, Lilly?" Erica asked.

"I'm spending Thanksgiving with Francis, my parents are out of town," Lilly replied with a twinge of regret. Maybe she should have gone home with Vincent.

Poor Lilly... Kathy's thoughts floated over her head.

"Let's hang out on Saturday or Sunday!" Kathy demanded.

Lilly quickly agreed as it gave her something to look forward to.

Despite all the cheeriness, Jen and Andy were finding plenty of time to fight, mainly about why Jen insisted on spending so much time with her family over the holiday.

At the end of the day they were wishing each other a happy Thanksgiving in the parking lot and leaving for the extended weekend when Quinn stopped her.

"Hey, uh, Lilly, have a great Thanksgiving."

"Thanks, Quinn," Lilly replied just as awkwardly.

"I was thinking, maybe you could tell me about it Friday at the movies."

"Uh..."

"Like a date." He quickly added, "I hear that movie about the singing football player is supposed to be really funny." Nervously, he rubbed the back of his neck.

Lilly caught Kathy mouthing *YES!* behind Quinn and found herself blurting out, "I'd love to!"

"Great, that's great, I'll text you the details!" He rushed off before she could change her mind.

Amir was waiting for him by his car; they fist bumped and blew it up.

CHAPTER 26

"It was written I should be loyal to the nightmare of my choice."
Joseph Conrad, Heart of Darkness

"Maybe we'll all crash your date tonight." Erica raised her eyebrows. "Do you know what movie you're seeing?"

Erica and Kathy insisted on coming over before her date to help her get ready. Neither of them could stay long, Kathy had a family thing and Erica was going Black Friday shopping with Dawn.

Lilly wasn't enjoying all the fuss, but Thanksgiving without her family had left her melancholy. She hadn't wanted to admit it, but she missed Emma and Vincent, and her dad.

Vincent had called her on Thanksgiving and it ended in a fight. Francis had tried to smooth it over by spending the whole day with her. He made them an enormous traditional Thanksgiving dinner; they watched the parade, then football, and movies all night until she passed out.

"The football comedy, thankfully not a sappy romance."

"That's no good, he has to see the girly side of you tonight, and girls like romance," Erica retorted. "He's picking you up right?" Erica took a break from overturning Lilly's closet.

"No, I'm meeting him there."

"Really, Lilly? Do you even want a second date? You have to make him feel like a man."

"It's fine," Kathy protested, waving Erica away.

Erica took a dress from the closet. "Perfect."

"No, no, no, come on it's kinda cold. Just jeans and a sweater or something. I'll let you do my makeup or hair. Just no short dress in this chilly weather." Lilly took the dress and shoved it back in the closet.

Erica groaned.

"Fine," Kathy glared.

"So, what does Francis think of your little date tonight?" Erica inquired.

"Not sure, he's pretty quiet."

"Heh." Erica was still looking through her closet. She found the box of her mom's clothes in the closet and sifted through it, while Kathy pinned Lilly's hair back.

"Hey, that's my mom's, don't mess with it…"

Erica nodded and moved onto her shoes. "Oh! We're the same size." Erica grinned.

Lilly patiently let Kathy work on her makeup and Erica tried on her shoes.

"I could, maybe, see myself dating Amir," Kathy admitted.

246

"Oh, you should!" Lilly said.

"He's cute," Erica added.

"But, I mean, if he isn't interested enough to ask me out after going through grade school together maybe it won't ever happen."

"Psh, ask him out!"

"Says the one who wants Lilly to show Quinn her feminine side?" Kathy laughed, throwing a shoe at Erica.

Lilly wasn't really listening. She was daydreaming about double dating and how fun it would be, but she reminded herself she wasn't sure she even liked Quinn. He was nice and cute and kind, but how could she even consider liking someone when she couldn't tell him who she really was?

Francis heard Lilly leaving her apartment and went to the door. Chamuel appeared before the door. She stood there, arms crossed, stronger than a stonewall before him. Fists formed and he turned away in anger, prepared to jump off the balcony if he had to. But Chamuel was in front of him again.

"Chamuel, why?"

She didn't respond. He turned and again Chamuel stood before him.

"It's going to happen tonight, isn't it? And yet you stop me from helping."

"Angels cannot interfere with destiny."

"I am angel no more!" He snapped.

Chamuel laughed. "You are still bound to us, brother." She touched a rune peering out from under his shirt. "You cannot interfere. Next time I will not be the one stopping you."

Chamuel was gone.

"There are always loopholes." Francis pulled a large worn book from his bookcase. "Aperio," he uttered and the bookshelf shifted away from the wall revealing Francis's artillery closet. Along with his weapons hung his golden chainmail armor, a twenty-pound bag of salt, and five-gallon jugs of holy water. "Time to prepare for battle."

He dialed a number on his phone. It rang a few times before a voice answered. "Thaddeus," Francis spoke into the phone. "I need a favor."

The theater in the mall was flooded with kids, all excited to have a few extra days off and packed in like sardines, making it louder than a cafeteria. Most adults were avoiding the mall altogether or just sticking to the more expensive stores and restaurants that weren't likely to draw in students.

Lilly didn't recognize most of them, she hadn't been in Wakefield long enough to know anyone.

Pushing through the clusters of people, she tried to find the back entrance Quinn had wanted to meet at. She guessed she was at the front and pushed her way towards the back.

The voices were bouncing off the tall walls to make one noisy jumble. All the pressure was getting to Lilly; her head felt like it was in a clamp, ready to explode any moment, so she moved faster. A humming noise ebbed from behind, compelling her to look back, but when she turned there was only a shadow out of place. It disappeared around the far corner. Lilly stared, debating following it. The humming grew louder.

She closed her eyes, giving herself a moment to calm her senses from the cafeteria-like environment. The humming elevated into a crescendo, and then stopped.

"Watch it!" A kid pushed her from behind. He looked as if she had somehow ruined his life and strutted away.

Lilly searched for the shadow, but saw nothing. Chalking it up to first date nerves, Lilly pushed through the back doors and sought out Quinn. It was just starting to drizzle and everyone pushed past her to get inside.

Just as the doors opened to the dark night sky, there was a flash of blue eyes, then green eyes to her left. Then red eyes on her right, but they moved so fast she couldn't see where they went or who they belonged to.

Lilly was frozen in place. Since she had gotten the sight from Iris she had seen a few strange things, but nothing like this.

"Lilly!" Quinn called to her. His voice released her from the concerning eyes; she must have been imagining things.

Quinn was across the street just getting out of his car.

Lilly was about to cross the street to him when it happened. Her foot was on the curb, ready to step into the street, when it felt like someone tapped her on the shoulder. In the same moment, Lilly's wrists felt like they were on fire. She clutched her left wrist, wincing.

"Lilly?" Quinn stared at her funny.

Whipping around, Lilly saw the shadow of a figure a few feet away. It was moving rapidly back into the movie theater, where it disappeared.

Then tires screeched and someone screamed.

Lilly quickly turned back to the road. Elaine was speeding with Derek was in the passenger's seat and another girl hanging out the sunroof. Not even a foot away from Lilly, Lyda was crossing the street. Elaine swerved and lost control of her car, the tires burning against the pavement trying to stop, but it was too late. The car hit Lyda; Lyda and Elaine were the ones screaming.

Quinn was already running to the scene, dialing 911 on his cell, and others flooded to the accident. Lilly would have run to them too, but she saw what they couldn't—that Lyda was already dead.

Lilly, unable to move, watched Lyda's spirit rise from her body. Lyda stared at Lilly helplessly while shadowy floating figures emerged from a hole in the sky that led to Abditus. The shadows consumed Lyda and as more pushed through Abditus, they spanned out across the theater parking lot.

To the left of the scene there were bright white orbs moving slowly towards Lyda's body. She felt the peace the orbs brought and knew they were angels. They beckoned her, "Leave this place, run, Lilly."

Then from the hole to Abditus emerged a dark pit of cloaked, red-eyed figures, even darker than the shadows. Demons. They encircled Lyda's body and soul. Lyda's pained eyes met Lilly's and cried out in terror. But before could take her, a flash of light burst into the center of the demons, scattering them.

One of the demons landed near Lilly. It stabled itself, then turned and stared at her, turning its head from side to side and slinking closer. Its face was black and nothing, but Lilly felt its evil piercing through her.

An angel crashed into the demon, sending it flying away, screeching. "Leave, before they come," the angel said.

Lilly turned to run and there stood Zeke at the doors to the theater, watching the accident unfold. He looked petrified as his eyes met Lilly's, and then he ran in the opposite direction. Lilly tore after him, not sure what she was going to do or say, but positive that all this was his fault.

Oddly enough, Zeke's face was red and he was sweating profusely. Not once had he broken a sweat in gym class and now he wasn't even running that fast. They were weaving in and out of groups of people, but Lilly was closing in on him.

Zeke looked back at her like *she* was the thing to be afraid of and ran into someone, knocking them both over. He jumped up from the ground, but not quick enough. Lilly grabbed him by his forearm and didn't let go.

"What have you done? Why Lyda?" Lilly's grip didn't falter. Her left hand rested on Sabriel in case he moved.

They stood face to face and he panted, "The contract, I had to seal the contract." Zeke stopped trying to get away and looked down. "It was her or me."

"What contract?" Lilly demanded.

"I'll explain, but we have to leave."

"Or what? We'll die?" She couldn't stop shouting at him.

"Yes, we will die. They're out for us now and if they catch us, we're dead." He nodded behind them. The shadows were seeping in the back doors of the theater and slowly making their way towards them, as the angels and demons continued to battle.

"What are the shadows?" Lilly asked.

"Spirits, empty lost souls, and the demons and angels of death follow close behind them. The spirits will slow us down if they catch us, but the angels and demons..."

Zeke's voice faded as the shadowy spirits neared.

Thaddeus emerged from the noisy crowd. He stood in front of Lilly and held his hands out towards the spirits, and angels, and demons behind them. Green beams of light escaped his palms and threw up some sort of force field the spirits could not pass. They ran into it continually, shaking the force field, but making no progress.

Lilly looked around; clearly no one else saw what they saw.

"Go!" Thaddeus bellowed. "Find Francis, and do not enter Abditus!" Thaddeus breathed heavily as he struggled. The spirits pushed against the force field and little by little Thaddeus was propelled backward.

Zeke grabbed Lilly's arm and to her surprise it didn't burn like it usually did. Even so, she left her feet planted in place, not sure if she could trust him.

"If we wait here, we're dead."

She didn't move, remembering Francis saying Zeke would get her killed.

"I know what Francis told you, but the contract is over. I'm free from its bindings," he pleaded.

He grabbed her by both arms just above the elbow. "Hold on." Zeke took a deep breath and his eyes rolled back in his head.

The next thing Lilly knew they were gliding through Abditus. But it wasn't smooth like when Raziel had flown her through it; everything around them blended together from moving so quickly. Her trip with Raziel had been a blink of an eye. The lights, colors, people, it was all one big dark blur with Zeke. The only thing that could be made out were the spirits, which seemed immersed in everything, and the angels and demons, but they were much further away, staring at Lilly and Zeke hungrily.

The demons called to them. Their bodies were like crippled, deteriorating creatures with bright red eyes. Some had tiny horns, others long fingernails more like talons, but most just looked like decrepit, infinitely furious creatures.

Most wore black cloaks that hung over their heads so all that could be seen were their eyes. Others left their hoods down so their heads, and even emaciated bodies, were exposed.

They landed in the parking lot, side by side in Zeke's car. By the time Lilly had recovered from the 15-second rollercoaster through Abditus, they were already burning rubber out of the parking lot.

"Breathe," he encouraged her.

She took a deep breath.

"Thaddeus said not to enter Abditus," Lilly scoffed.

"It was the fastest way to get out of there," Zeke snapped, rapidly tapping his fingers against the steering wheel.

"Why did you do it, Zeke?"

"That wasn't how it was supposed to go."

Her eyes narrowed, glaring at him.

"You were supposed to die, OK?" He retorted. "But you didn't, you wouldn't let me influence you. Then you saw me and I had to make a distraction so I could get away."

"So you killed an innocent girl and you meant to kill me? Wonderful! Let me out, Zeke."

"You don't understand. Lyda will go to heaven, I'm sure of it, but if they catch me, I'd be tortured in hell for all of eternity for breaking my contract and letting my mark, you, see me! And if they catch you…" Zeke sped up through a yellow light.

"What if they catch me?"

"We need a safe house." He pressed a few buttons on his phone.

"Francis," Lilly urged.

Zeke shook his head. "Skoal," he said when the phone was picked up. "It's all gone wrong. I couldn't influence her, she wouldn't do it." His voice was desperate.

"They're after you?" Skoal asked.

"Yes, they're after me, and Lilly too."

"She's with you?"

"Yes, I couldn't just let them take her! What do I do, where can we go to elude them?"

"Not here. Don't you dare bring them here!"

Zeke did a quick u-turn. "Then where do I go, Skoal? Do I just let them take us? Would you like it if I just gave up?"

"No Zeke, I would have liked it if you listened to me in the first place and didn't sign the contract. Now you have to live with your decision! I'm sorry, I can't help you."

The car swerved as Zeke slammed the phone down next to him.

"Francis's place?"

"No."

"Yes! Thaddeus said to go to Francis."

"Francis... He hates me, he wouldn't let me in."

"That's just it though, isn't it? You're not *allowed* in, right?"

"Of course. His apartment is safeguarded against those of the other side..."

Again they changed direction and after a blur of red and green lights they finally pulled up at the apartments. As soon as they got out of the car, Zeke grabbed Lilly by the arm.

"What are you doing?" She attempted to pull away.

"Just in case we have to Fade again."

He looked in every direction as they made their way into the building. Lilly wondered what things he may see that her sight failed to show her. The second he knocked on Francis's door, the dogs were growling. Francis swung the door open; bat in hand, wearing his chainmail armor.

"Come in, Lilly."

Lilly stepped in and he was ready to slam the door in Zeke's face, but Lilly put her foot in front of the door.

"You have to let Zeke in."

"No, I don't."

Lilly didn't budge.

"Did you break the contract?" Francis growled at Zeke.

"Yes and no, she didn't take to my influencing, then she saw me, so they're after both of us now." Zeke looked down like a little boy that spilled his milk, then smeared it into the carpet trying to clean it up.

"You can come in," Francis said grudgingly.

CHAPTER 27

"It is a fact verified and recorded in many histories that the soul capable of the greatest good is also capable of the greatest evil."

John Steinbeck

The dogs didn't stop growling until Francis chastised them, not because he didn't want them to growl, but because the sound was starting to irritate him. Francis and Lilly sat next to each other and Zeke in the chair across from them, even though Lilly wanted to sit across from *them* and grill them for answers.

"Since the contract is broken, we should--" Francis continued talking just to Zeke.

"Is someone going to tell me what this contract is or are you two going to continue to talk about it without enlightening me?" Lilly snapped.

"Well..." Zeke started.

"You have to tell me, I don't even know why I'm being hunted by demons!"

"Technically as the Keeper, every demon should want to hunt you," Zeke replied.

Francis shot Zeke a death stare. "You--" he shouted.

"I'll tell her, it's my fault." Zeke threw his hands up apologetically. "As a Half Life I'm obliged to sign contracts--"

"You can choose which to sign. You're only required to read them if you're called," Francis interrupted.

"Yes, I can choose, but it's part of who I am. I'm supposed to be contracted."

Francis snorted.

"And yes, it's my choice if I contract with an angel or demon, but this time I chose to work with a demon. That was my decision, I own up to that. I signed a contract, before I met you Lilly, to influence you to do dumb little things, but you would never do any of them."

Francis listened closely.

"The demon Gahdarina, Gahd, she contracted me. It was supposed to end tonight. I was supposed to influence you to yell at Quinn for being late, and thus walk into the road and get hit by the car...and..."

"And die?"

"Yes."

"But you couldn't influence me."

"No. You never listen."

"She doesn't," Francis agreed.

"If I couldn't influence her I was supposed to kill her myself, but I couldn't kill you. That's why... I'm sorry about Lyda, but I had to. I needed a distraction, since I didn't fulfill my contract, so I could hide."

"What happened to Lyda?"

"She's dead…" Tears were in Lilly's eyes.

"You bastard," Francis was on his feet, ready to strangle him.

Zeke stood prepared to fight, his hands extended in front of him to push Francis back with his energy.

"Francis, stop! We need a plan." Lilly stood between them. "It won't do any good to kill him now," she added when he didn't move.

Francis snorted, but backed down just the same.

"How long will they hunt us?"

"They might stop hunting you if he's dead," Francis motioned to Zeke.

Lilly glared at him. Somehow she doubted that.

"Only for a day," Francis replied. "For twenty-four hours you'll be on the radar, your souls exposed in Abditus for the taking."

Lilly and Zeke listened intently.

"Usually, your spirit is dim and undistinguishable, but when you break a deal like this you're bright as day as if your human form is in Abditus, glowing. They'll know where you are from miles away. The savage part of being an angel, they have to hunt people like you, Lilly. Take their lives away, just to keep them," he gestured to Zeke, "from getting you."

261

"I'm *not* a demon."

Francis ignored him and continued, "They're going to use this to get to the sword, Lilly. You have to find it first. It's the best way to get them off your heels. If you already possess it, they can't take it from you."

"We've gone over this. I have no idea where it is, Francis. My mom never told me."

Zeke gasped, "Then it's true, the Ferryman does exist."

Francis faced him. "You're a fool for signing that contract. Gahd will tear you to shreds when she finds you."

"That's easy for you to say, you're a *perfect* angel!"

"If I was perfect, would I have jumped and chosen a life of imperfection?"

"Wait, what about the oracle?" Lilly said before they could start again.

They both stared at her, confused.

"The oracle, can't it tell me where the Ferryman is?"

"She's right!" Zeke agreed. "But Sybil is missing, and Seymour is in hiding, no one knows where he is."

"I know where Sybil is." Francis glared at Zeke accusingly.

"What?" Zeke was perplexed. "Skoal and I have been looking for Sybil ourselves, to help me out of this mess…"

"Your friend, Samael--" Francis started.

But there was a banging on the door. The dogs jumped up and sniffed around the cracks of the door, wagging their tails.

"Yes?" Francis opened the door impatiently.

"Do you know the girl who lives across from you, Lilly?" Vincent's voice echoed across the apartment.

"Vincent." Francis opened the door wide enough for Vincent to see Lilly.

"Yeah, how'd you know?" Vincent stepped in and glanced between Lilly, Zeke, and Francis. "Lilly." Vincent was well over six feet tall with an athletic build and green eyes. He looked goofy in his suit and tie, and his dress shoes looked more like clown shoes. He stood there in the doorway, consuming it. "Lilly. It's so good to see you. I can't believe you're really here, in Wakefield." Vincent crossed the room and hugged her.

Francis shut the door.

"I, uh, it's good to see you too, Vin, but really this is about the worst time you could visit."

"You're with friends." He nodded. "I'm sure they don't mind." His good mood was contagious even with the high tension of the situation at hand. "You look so familiar." He gestured to Francis.

"Francis Wills." They shook hands.

"Vincent Guthrie." Vincent looked at Francis's strange attire, then shrugged and drew his attention back to Lilly. "You look great, Lil! I just flew in from Dad's..."

Before he could say more, a buzzing sound distracted everyone from the conversation. The buzzing turned into a loud hum and a gold flash of light emerged from the window. Out of the light came Iris.

"Iris," Francis uttered.

"We have to leave, quick, there's a Succubus headed this way." Iris was out of breath. "Who knows what else they have released."

"What's going on?" Vincent was backing away to the door, in awe at the sudden appearance of Iris.

"The two of you need to go with Iris, now, as fast as you can." Francis nodded to Zeke and Lilly.

"But they'll just follow us wherever we go. Where could we run?" Zeke questioned.

"Gabriel is on his way. He was hoping to find you first, but in the mean time you have me..." Iris put out her arms for Zeke and Lily to take.

Zeke looked at Iris questioningly.

"Messengers," Lilly remembered from training, "are veiled from demons *and* angels." Lilly grabbed hold of Iris's arm. Zeke followed suit with the news Iris could save them.

"Demon? Angels? This is crazy, Lilly, let's go."

Vincent reached for Lilly, but Francis grabbed him. Vin tried to break free of Francis's grip, with no avail.

"But if Gabriel gets to us first..." Zeke's words quieted.

Francis's eyes widened at the fear in Zeke's voice.

"Wait, contract him." Francis broke Iris's hold on Lilly and Zeke.

"Good thinking. James Ezekiel Russo, I contract you to protect Lilly with your life and help her find the Ferryman, for the next twenty-four hours that you are hunted."

Iris took Lilly's dagger and sliced her palm. She handed it to Zeke, who followed suit. Iris held her hand out to him and everyone held their breath. Zeke hesitated once before gripping her hand firmly. He closed his eyes and when they opened again they were blue.

"We have to go." Iris grabbed Lilly.

"Lilly!" Vin shouted as they Faded.

No sooner had the left, the apartment shook, lights flickering and the dogs were growling.

"What the Hell? Where did they take my sister?"

"Hell is exactly it." Francis brushed past Vincent. "I'm really sorry Vincent, but we'll have to catch up later." Francis reached his open palm out and his energy pushed Vincent back into the bedroom. Vincent's arms flailed and he shouted, but

265

the door slammed and a chair wedged itself between the floor and the door handle. Vin shouted and attempted to break down the door until there was a loud crashing sound and he went silent.

The noise was all the windows in the apartment shattering with the gust of wind that carried in the Succubus. She landed on the balcony and looked at the warding around the balcony doorframe. She laughed and tore the entire doorframe off, tossing it into the road like it was a paperweight. She stepped into the living room.

She was sickly skinny, not someone you would expect to be strong, but with the slightest movement of her arms, her toned muscles showed through dying skin. Standing as tall as the ceiling would allow, her dirty blonde hair was down to her waist and she wore a sleeveless back shirt and tight leather pants with nothing on her feet.

Francis grabbed his bat, pressing the grip end of the bat against his hand. Long shiny golden spikes sprang out of the head of the bat. Cuff and Link snarled at his side, ready to attack.

"Gold from mount Ebal, laced with angel hair. And familiars…" The Succubus licked her lips. "Impressive."

"I hope you have something equally as impressive." Francis held his bat up high ready to strike.

"You're looking at it," replied the Succubus as it struck.

CHAPTER 28

"Run from what's comfortable. Forget safety. Live where you fear to live. Destroy your reputation. Be notorious. I have tried prudent planning long enough. From now on I'll be mad."

Jalaluddin Rumi

Iris landed them in Zeke's car, set perfectly in the seats. Going through Abditus with Iris was much more pleasant and quick. Lilly barely noticed it happened at all. Lilly snapped her seatbelt on as Zeke spiraled into the road without even looking. Lilly looked around for Iris, but didn't see her.

"She's on the roof." Zeke nodded as he turned onto the highway.

Lilly looked up and noticed a golden glow on the roof.

"Just keeping an eye out." Iris stuck her head through the roof of the car.

Lilly jumped at the sight of Iris's intact head sticking through the roof.

"Sorry," she smiled, "few forces can hold me." With that she popped her head back through. Lilly imagined her sitting on the roof Indian style just enjoying the beauty of the night.

"She's probably laying flat on her back." Zeke weaved in and out of cars on the highway.

"Oh great, you too," Lilly snapped. "Don't listen to my thoughts!"

"That would be hard, since you yell in your head."

"I'm sure you'll figure it out. Or a few more lessons with Jophiel... Where are we going, anyway?"

"To my friend Samael in Virginia. Francis seems to think Sam has the oracle, Sybil. If he does, we can find the Ferryman. If not, we can stay with him until this death sentence is over."

"Just twenty-four hours, that shouldn't be too hard."

"Not if Gabriel finds us," Zeke retorted.

"And what's bad about an angel finding us? Gabriel is really very nice."

Zeke snorted and shook his head. "If Gabriel finds us we're dead, just the same as if a demon finds us."

"That's ridiculous, why would an angel kill us?" She leaned towards him. "Gabriel is my friend, Zeke."

"To keep us out of Hell. As a friend, Gabriel would keep you out of Hell, even if that means your death."

"Then why not just protect us for twenty-four hours?"

"Too risky," Iris's voice buzzed from outside.

"They will choose the sword over you, Lilly," Zeke sighed.

"The sword in the hands of demons would mean the end of times," Iris retorted.

"The sooner we get to Sam's, the better."

"And why not go through Abditus with Iris?"

"Too risky," Iris said.

Lilly groaned, leaning back and submitting to the next few hours in the car. At least with Iris they were off the radar to angels and demons alike. Even so, she kept her hand rested on Sabriel in case Zeke or Iris failed her.

Every so often, Iris would pop her head through the roof and let them know there was an accident ahead, the right lane was a little clearer to go through, or they needed to reroute to avoid a lurking demon.

As Lilly dozed off, she tried to think where her mom would have hidden the Ferryman, but all she could think of were the night's events. Screeching tires, the spirits, the red eyes, Thaddeus, and poor Lyda.

Clunk, clunk… ca clunk, clunk, clunk.

Lilly's eyes shot open to see hail the size of golf balls pelting the windshield.

Iris stuck her head through the roof. "Lex," she panted. "He's found us."

"What should I do?" Zeke slowed down a bit.

"Try to outrun him. He won't be able to see us for long if I can concentrate hard enough." She disappeared.

That was all Zeke needed to hear. He pushed his foot so hard on the pedal they swerved. He let up on the gas, and they cruised down the highway faster than Lilly imagined a car could go.

"Lex?"

"Lex is a Lix; a weather demon. Thus the hail." Zeke motioned toward the windshield.

"How does he know where we are? I thought Iris--"

"I lost my concentration, thank you." Iris snorted as she emerged again. "Now give me a moment and I'll--OW" A ball of ice fell through the roof after pelting Iris in the head. She grabbed it off the seat next to Lilly and threw it out of the car. "As I was saying, if you'll be patient, we'll be out of this spot in a moment." Her head jolted back out.

Lilly lay her head against the window and rubbed her temples.

"Your head hurts?"

"Just a bit," she mumbled sarcastically.

"Put your seat back and sleep a while." He placed his hand on Lilly's shoulder and she felt a command of sleepy peacefulness fall over her.

"I see you can manage the angel part of your Half Life as well," Lilly yawned.

Zeke's face twisted as he thought about her words.

It only took a few moments after she reclined to drift off to sleep.

The night was quiet again; everything was dark, except for the headlights of the car and the bright stars up above. Lilly woke, blinking a few times and focused on the driver's side. Zeke was still speeding, but from the looks of the road, they weren't on the highway anymore, but a two-lane road surrounded by trees.

Zeke smiled over at her, then concentrated back at the road. He looked so old in that instant, Lilly couldn't figure out how anyone thought he was young enough to be in high school. His brow was wrinkled and his face looked uncomfortable as it contorted into a defined thinking pose.

She blinked again and realized only one of his hands clutched to the wheel. Following his arm, Lilly found his other hand was grasping hers. Surprised and uncomfortable, she let her hand go limp in his. She had been trying to block her thoughts from him, but before she drifted off to sleep again, she swore he dropped his icy concentration and smirked.

CHAPTER 29

"Though a good deal is too strange to be believed, nothing is too strange to have happened."

Thomas Hardy

Vincent kicked the door once more and cursed. The windows in the bedroom had burst just after he was flung into the room, leaving shattered glass all around the room. There were still noises clearly defining a struggle on the other side of the door. He searched the room, trying to find something that might help him break the door down, but the room was simple. A small bed, nightstand with a few books, a lamp, and a very well organized closet that hung open.

When Vincent looked back to the door, Suriel stood in front of him. Vincent gasped and took a step back. The back of his knees hit the bed and he fell back onto it.

"What the…"

Suriel smiled. She was sporting her war garb, like Francis, golden chest plate and purple tunic underneath, with leather sandals. Her beautiful dark hair was gathered on one side and her wings were outstretched over her shoulders, not even near full span.

"What's going on?"

"It's time to remember, Vincent." Suriel placed her hand on Vincent's forehead before he had a chance to stop her.

His eyes closed as the memories came flooding back to him. Every time Francis had gotten him out of the house while his mom was sick. Francis teaching him to fight, Jophiel reading him books in a very dark place, and Suriel standing guard at his bedroom door, night after night, as his mother screamed. Vincent pushed her hand away.

"No. I don't want to remember, Suriel." He shook his head. "I want to go back to school, not to worry about all this." His head kept shaking back and forth.

He knew what Francis was doing now; he was fighting a demon. Something Vincent had seen his fair share of in his childhood. He was finally getting back to normalcy, not this...

"I was done with this, everyone agreed. Why bring me back now?" Vincent's voice was filled with resentment.

"It is your destiny. Remember." Suriel's hand raised to Vincent's forehead again. This time it was too much and he passed out.

Jophiel appeared at Suriel's side with his sword drawn. "More are coming."

Suriel drew her sword and they both faced the shattered windows, waiting.

Francis pulled his sword from the chest of the Succubus lying motionless on the floor. As she made gargling noises,

274

Francis swung his sword over his head and let it fall across her neck.

Gabriel and Raziel appeared on either side of Francis.

"More?" Francis asked as he cleaned his sword.

"At least two legions. They're swarming Abditus, finding any way they can to get here. Michael called two-thirds of the Powers in to battle," Raziel stated grimly.

"Where is Lilly?" Gabriel asked.

"With Iris."

"Where?"

Francis shrugged.

"You know." Gabriel hulked over him.

"Your orders are to take her. I will not let that happen."

Gabriel made a move to force Francis to tell him, but there was a crash and suddenly giant, bare, lizard-like demons surrounded them.

Raziel cracked his staff against the floor and they were transported to Abditus, where even more demons surrounded them. In every direction there were at least two demons to every angel fighting.

"Go," Raziel ordered Gabriel.

Gabriel nodded and he was gone with one swish of his wings.

"Ready?" Raziel questioned, loosening his knees as he took to battle stance.

"I call the big one." Francis pointed out a horned demon three times his size.

"Just like old times." Raziel's deep voice echoed as he lashed out at the charging demons.

CHAPTER 30

"A person often meets his destiny on the road he took to avoid it."

Jean de La Fontaine, Fables

The car eased to a stop and the engine muttered after Zeke took the key out of the ignition. It was the dead of night; the sun would rise in a few hours. Zeke was opening her door when Lilly woke. It was nearly impossible to see the small two-level farmhouse covered in vines at the end of a gravel driveway, save for the glow of the moon. All around them were fields and woods, and darkness.

"Where's Iris?" She stepped out and took a deep breath of cool country air.

"I asked her to leave before we got here."

"Leave? Why? They'll find us!"

"Calm down. I had to ask her to leave, otherwise Gabriel..." Zeke shook his head. "I'm not ready to die, and I don't know about you--"

"I'm not either."

"Then understand, if Iris stayed with us she may have let Gabriel find us. As long as we don't enter Abditus we're safe."

She nodded as they walked to the front door. "Do you have any power against them?"

277

"A little, enough to keep a few from us, but not many."

"Me too."

A smile emerged on Zeke's face.

The door was white with old cracked paint crumbling off it. The house itself looked like it should be condemned.

Zeke knocked three times on the front door, then paused and knocked twice more. The door swung open so hard Lilly thought it would put a hole in the wall, but it stopped before it hit. The doorway stood empty for a few seconds, then a shadowed figure appeared.

"Ezekiel!" Samael smiled.

"Sam."

Samael emerged and put his arms around Zeke, revealing himself in the moonlight. He had light brown hair that fell just over his ears, a short well-kept beard, and a crooked nose that cast a shadow from the light. The collar was popped on his light green polo and a tan cloth belt held up his washed out jeans, making him look like a beach bum, not a country boy.

"It's good to see you, Sam." Zeke patted him on the back.

"And who is this?"

"This is Lilly. Lilly, Samael. Let's skip the pleasantries and step inside," Zeke said hastily.

"All this time, and you come back now, in trouble?" Samael sat a cup of coffee down in front of Zeke. "You're sure you don't want any?" He asked Lilly.

"Positive," Lilly replied.

The inside of the house was filled with enormous wooden armchairs with high backs, a bamboo chest, and detailed cedar bookshelves the reached the ceilings. The wood floors were almost completely covered by elaborate Persian rugs.

They sat around a long mahogany dining table that could seat at least twelve people. Zeke and Samael sat across from each other, but with the size of the table there was still quite a few feet between them. Lilly sat at the head of the table near the living room.

"I thought I could trust you." Zeke sipped his coffee.

"I'm happy to have company. Even company with baggage." Samael's eyes darted to Lilly as he spoke. "Not too many contracts out here, not enough people. But that's what I wanted when I gave up my post."

"Sam used to do what I do at Wakefield," Zeke told Lilly.

"Ah." She nodded uncomfortably. They talked like two old fishing buddies, except the fish were people.

"I called you, even came here a few weeks back."

"Ah, just been off the grid, enjoying *life*." Samael laughed. "I'm glad we can catch up now, though."

"Yeah."

"You came for more than just a safe house though, didn't you?"

"Sybil," Zeke said.

Samael looked directly into Zeke's eyes.

"Why is she here?" Zeke asked.

"Ask the angels." Samael shrugged and leaned back in his chair. "I just do what they say."

Zeke's eyes narrowed and they stared at each other like they were having an entire conversation without a word.

Lilly searched the air above them for their thoughts, but there were none. The red in both their eyes flared up and Lilly's wrists blazed for an instant. She immediately regretted trusting Zeke.

Samael broke their gaze and Faded, only to reappear across the room with his hand on the door to another room.

"Come on, Lilly." Samael winked, taking a key ring from his pocket and unlocking the door.

"Come on." Zeke took her by the arm, pulling her from her seat. Being a Half Life made him impossibly strong compared to Lilly, but she imagined Suriel could kick his butt.

She placed her hand on Sabriel and nudged Zeke. He immediately let her go.

"You'll have to go in alone." Samael's voice was stern as he opened the door.

"That's fine." Lilly honestly had no idea what to expect.

Without warning, Samael shoved her in the room, slamming the door behind her.

The room was pitch black; Lilly couldn't even see her hands in front of her face. She heard the door lock behind her. There was no light coming in from the cracks of the door, because there were no cracks. Her heart raced and she closed her eyes only to realize that she wasn't sure if they were open or closed.

Just a few feet away a light turned on. Instinctively, she covered her eyes and let the bright light ease in. Pupils readjusted, she lowered her hands. There was just enough light to see the woman, and a little of what was in between them. The room appeared endless in the dark outside the light.

"I thought I heard a heartbeat," squeaked the woman.

With her back hunched over she was very short and her long unkempt silver hair traveled down past her waist. Despite her looks, her voice was young and lively, and her skin hardly wrinkled. A big blue bow sat at the top of her head and her large white shirt with billowing sleeves made it difficult to imagine her actual body shape. Her wavy skirt matched her bow and was just short enough to miss scraping against the wood floors.

"Sybil?"

"Yes, yes, and you're Lilly. Names are hardly a challenge." Sybil waved Lilly over.

Lilly took a step closer. In front of Sybil was a large table with instruments and cards strewn across it.

"You wish to know about your mom," Sybil said plainly.

"Yes." Lilly took another step.

"But they," Sybil nodded towards the door, "wish to know where the sword is."

"Yes! Where is it? Do you know?" Lilly was just across the table from her now.

"Only one, you must choose which one." Sybil fiddled with the objects on her table.

"But…" Lilly's face contorted. "I… I can find the sword on my own. What really happened to my mom?"

"Good choice." She paused, staring directly into Lilly's eyes. "Now let's see. How to do it… Spirit board…" She tossed the thin wood board with the alphabet and symbols carved into it so far across the room that by the time it hit the floor there was no light to prove it was even there. "Cartomancy, tarot…" Sybil pushed a few decks of cards with pictures and some with symbols on them to the back of the table. Some slipped off the back edge, but she paid no attention.

Lilly leaned over and picked up one of the cards that fell from the table. The card had a dark cloaked figure on it and 'Mortem' in big black curved letters across the top.

"Well, that's bad." Sybil stared at the card.

"What are *their* intensions?" Lilly's voice trembled. "Why did they send me in here?"

"For answers of course." Sybil continued to search. "Tasseography." She cackled and slapped a large teacup onto the floor, shattering it.

Lilly looked back down at the card. A spider crawled up from the back of it towards her fingers. "Ah!" She threw the card and rubbed her arms to get it off, but it was already gone.

"That won't keep them away. No horary or astromancy," She pushed through a stack of papers with symbols inside shapes and lines cutting through them from this side to that. She pushed a pendulum that hung over the papers out of the way. Her face grew annoyed as she stood over her table with her hands on her hips.

"Casting bones!" Sybil shouted excitedly and looked around. "Damn, no bones." Slowly, she stared up at Lilly's arms, biting her lip.

Lilly wiggled uncomfortably and snuck her arms behind her back the best she could.

"No, no, that won't work!" Sybil threw her hands in the air. She looked into Lilly's eyes like she was seeing her for the first time, her eyes seeping into Lilly's. Sybil's head cocked to the side and she grinned in such a way, her nostrils flared and her eyes glazed over, like she wasn't really looking at Lilly anymore.

"My dear, you're beaming." She strode towards Lilly like she was floating on a cloud. "Cheiromancy..." Her eyes were unblinking. "It won't even take that much..." She drew closer.

Lilly found herself backing away.

"Just a touch, that's all I'll need. I can practically read you from here." Extending her arm, she slid her bony fingers over Lilly's hands and clutched her wrist so tight Lilly could feel knuckle scrape carpals.

Lilly tried to get away, but the old woman wasn't old at all; she was quite strong. Sybil's body tremored, her eyes flipped back in her head, exposing only the whites of her eyes.

"Seven years, seven years today. Only three more," Sybil muttered.

With a jolt, Sybil was back, pupils showing again. She stared sympathetically, her eyes glazed with whatever she had seen. She took Lilly's wrists in her hands. "Misery burns these wrists, misery burns this heart, mind, and soul."

Her sharp nails scraped over the scar on Lilly's wrist. "I could take it out if you like? Just one deep, quick slice and you'll feel better when they're near." Blood started to pool from Lilly's skin where Sybil's fingernail rested.

"No!" Lilly jerked her wrists away.

"Very well." Sybil stared. "Still beaming...just beaming. You should at least see though," she said as she grabbed Lilly's arm.

CHAPTER 31

"The uptorn trees are not rooted again; the parted hills are left scarred… the hills underneath their green vesture bear the marks of the past rending. To the eyes that have dwelt on the past, there is no thorough repair."

George Eliot, The Mill on the Floss

When Lilly opened her eyes again, they were back in Adrian, in Lilly's old home. Her room looked almost the same as it did the day she left, except for the crib.

"Go on," Sybil nudged, her face still sympathetic to Lilly's circumstance.

The crib was tucked away in the corner near the bed. Lilly stepped closer to it. Leaning over the edge of the crib, Lilly saw there laid a sleeping baby. On the headboard of the crib Lilly noticed the ᚹ rune carved into it.

"Wunjo." Lilly touched it, then looked down at the baby. "Me?" Lilly asked Sybil.

"Yes."

Abruptly, the room shook and the lights flickered. With a simple sound like the lighting of a match, a demon emerged from the wood floors. The cloaked creature glowed green from the fire below it and crept to the edge of the crib.

"What's it doing?" Lilly whispered, backing away.

"Watch."

Lilly felt its presence so filled with hate, she grew anxious and irritable, despite knowing it was only a memory.

It leaned over the crib.

"Hush," it croaked in a low deep voice as it drew its fingernails over baby Lilly's skin. "Hush…"

Suddenly, it looked right up at Lilly, red eyes burning from the black depths of the cloak. Then with the subtlest of movements, it grinned within the darkness of its hood, turned back to baby Lilly and sliced the sides of her wrists with its fingernails. A green smoke emitted from the demon's fingers and the smoke entered baby Lilly's wrists.

Lilly clutched her own wrists that burned as if the demon was poisoning her again. She tried not to scream because she feared the demon would *notice* her again if she did; fearing even in the memory it could harm her.

Baby Lilly cried and in a matter of seconds Eva ran in, the Ferryman strapped to her back. She stopped dead at the doorway and stared into the eyes of the demon. It grinned at Eva and Faded as soon as she reached for the Ferryman.

Eva ran to the crib and scooped up baby Lilly in her arms. She tried her best to calm her and keep the baby from crying, but she didn't stop. An angel appeared with a golden light glowing behind him, making it hard to see him. He rested his green glowing staff against the wall.

Eva lay the baby back in the crib.

"She's been marked." His voice was calm, but apologetic.

"What do I do?" Eva let out a quiet cry.

"You'll save her at any cost?"

"Yes."

"Place your hands on her wrists, gently, and I'll do the rest." The angel watched as Eva complied. Then he placed his hands over her mother's. There was a jolt as the green smoke left the baby, passed over the angel and onto Eva.

The baby stopped crying, but Eva passed out.

The angel caught her and helped her up onto the bed.

"Forgive me," the angel said before he Faded.

Sybil grabbed Lilly by the arm again and they spun and turned until they were back in her dark hole of a room.

Sybil hobbled to her table, lazily sifting through things.

"The demon was trying to kill me, not her."

Sybil shrugged. "C'est la vie."

"The green, it was cancer..."

Sybil stared into her crystal ball, leaning in more and more, not hearing anything Lilly said.

"It's my fault..."

Sybil's nose was only a few centimeters away from the crystal ball when she finally stopped.

"Twice," Sybil muttered, then stepped back from the ball. "At least twice!"

The next thing Lilly knew Sybil was right in front of her, arms outreached and grabbing for Lilly's shoulders.

"Twice!"

Swiftly, Lilly backed away, but Sybil was there with her every step she took. Lilly's back cracked as she accelerated into the door.

Sybil continued to shout and shake her as Lilly slid down the door.

"Zeke!" She screamed, jiggling the door handle.

"That's it, Zeke." Sybil stopped.

"What?"

"Zeke. Twice. Zeke will defy you twice, at least. It could be more. We can't really say, things can change. But twice, he will, that's a fact. He'll try to kill you among your peers--"

"At the theater?"

"Yes, yes, the theater!" She stared at Lilly as if she had some secret sight.

"That's already happened."

On the other side of the door keys rattled. Someone was working the handle.

Sybil leaned down an inch from Lilly's own nose, "Then once more, Lilly Guthrie. He'll try to kill you once more. He can't be trusted." Her features were maddening.

The door fell out from behind her and Lilly was again in Samael's living room. Samael stood over her and Sybil continued her quest to get as close as possible to Lilly, until he stopped her.

Lilly crawled backwards into Zeke's legs. She sat motionless, staring up at him.

Samael grabbed Sybil and thrust her up from the ground. He whispered a few words in her ear and Sybil hobbled back into the dark room. Samael locked the door behind her.

"Why keep her locked up?" Lilly asked.

"To keep her safe." Samael hooked the keys back on his belt loop. "Without Seymour she's near mad, and out in the elements alone... *Someone* would be bound to pick her up and use her for the wrong thing."

"Oh."

Zeke helped Lilly to her feet.

"You OK?" He asked

"Yeah."

Lilly brushed him off, remembering Sybil's words. She immediately regretted the thought; perhaps he would kill her right then and there if he knew that she knew. But Zeke didn't make any implication that he heard her thoughts. *Thanks, Jophiel.*

"What did she say?" Samael asked.

Lilly shook her head.

"We let you see her, now what did she say?" Samael stood right in front of her, puffing his chest out, his eyes red.

Lilly's mouth fell open, unable to speak and too numb to notice her wrists.

"Hey, Sam." Zeke tried to get between them, but Samael didn't budge or break his gaze from Lilly. "Samael!" Zeke pushed him and a small jolt forced Samael back.

They exchanged a look, Zeke trying to determine his friend's angle.

Lilly stood angry and deceived. *Francis was right,* Lilly thought, *a Half Life couldn't be trusted.*

Sam shrugged and sat back at the dining room table. Light was emanating from behind the curtains; the sun was up.

"How long was I in there?"

"A good while," Sam replied nonchalantly.

"You look tired, you should sleep a while," Zeke said. He took a pillow and blanket form the bamboo chest and placed them on the sofa.

Lying down, Lilly closed her eyes and planned her escape. If Sybil wasn't completely crazy, Lilly might die tonight by the hand of the Half Life contracted to protect her.

CHAPTER 32

"I do know that the slickest way to lie is to tell the right amount of truth--then shut up."
Robert A. Heinlein, Stranger in a Strange Land

"She's the real deal, isn't she?" Samael said once he was sure Lilly had fallen asleep.

"What?" Zeke sipped his coffee.

He really didn't even need the stuff, well, maybe his human side did, but as long as he kept himself at the top of his game, he wouldn't fall into the weaknesses of being human.

Zeke and Samael were watching Lilly and the four guard angels who surrounded her.

"She's the Keeper of the sword. The Ferryman is real."

"How do you know about the sword?" Zeke sat his mug down.

"Everyone knows the legend, Zeke," Samael scoffed.

"You lie." Zeke raised his voice as much as he dared to.

"Look at her!" Samael's fist hit the table. "Four guardian angels, watching over her—just her—while she sleeps. I've never seen that before. Have you?"

Zeke was silent. He took a moment to watch Lilly again.

Samael stood and took his keys from his pocket, swinging them around. "There's something more to her than just the sword. I bet you Gahd knows."

Zeke snorted. Just the thought of Gahd made his blood boil human again. Gahd had gotten him into this mess.

Zeke stared at the angels around Lilly. They didn't face her to comfort her, but away from her; they were a wall to keep the unwanted out. They wore battle garb Zeke hadn't seen an angel wear for a very long time. Except for Francis, Francis was wearing nearly the exact same thing when they arrived at his apartment the night before.

A tiny spark inside his brain told him exactly what he needed to know.

"You wanna talk to Sybil?" Samael broke Zeke's train of thought. He motioned to the door that held Sybil in.

"No..." Zeke stood up and stretched. "I think I'll get a little shut eye."

"You sure?"

"Yeah."

"Your human side must be worn out," Samael chuckled and put the keys away again. "Let me know if you need anything." Samael Faded.

Zeke walked over to Lilly. He had to lean over the angels to even look at her. When he leaned, they leaned. Zeke stared at one, frustrated to the core, but the angel didn't blink; it knew its job.

Zeke leaned in close to one of the guardians. "Samael, he deceives me?" Zeke whispered quietly.

"Yes," the angel replied, but all four angels nodded solemnly in unison.

"We need Iris." No sooner had the words left his lips, did one of the angels disappear. "Do we wait for Iris?"

"No." The guardian shook his head and then he knelt down and shook Lilly's shoulder.

Lilly's eyes burst open and she stared at the unknown angel. He put a finger over his mouth signaling her to stay quiet.

"Go with Zeke," he said, before disappearing from Lilly's sight.

Lilly stared at Zeke confused.

"Sam can't be trusted," he whispered.

Before she could question him, Zeke touched her and they Faded to his car once more. Placing his hand on the dashboard he started the engine, but it was quiet.

"Another plus of being a Half Life." Zeke smiled.

"Oh, and I was afraid you could only manipulate *people*," Lilly said groggily.

Zeke rolled his eyes as they slowly pulled out of the driveway, but once back on the main road he floored it.

"We have to find the Ferryman, it's--"

"Zeke, I don't know where it is!" Lilly snapped.

"Sybil didn't know?"

"I—I don't know." Lilly crossed her arms. "Why can't we trust Sam?"

"Sam is working for Gahd, your guardians confirmed it."

"Oh... OH."

"I wouldn't be surprised if we just missed Gahd."

"Wait, my guardians?"

"Yes. You have four guardian angels with you, always."

"Here, now?" Lilly looked around. "I don't see..."

Zeke nodded. "You can't see them, unless they want you to. All but one, one is getting Iris."

Lilly looked in the rear view mirror and noticed an angel sitting in the back seat. When she turned the angel was gone.

"Well, that's comforting." Lilly rested her head back, content to stay with Zeke if her guardian angels were there.

Sam looked out the second floor window of his house and watched as Lilly and Zeke drove away. He sat back down in his chair and Gahd Faded in behind him.

"So?"

"They just left, Gahd."

"Where to?"

"Headed north again."

"And the sword?"

"Lilly wouldn't say what Sybil told her, but she was distressed after talking to her. I'm sure she knows where it is."

"She'd better," Gahd threatened and then Faded.

CHAPTER 33

"It's no use going back to yesterday, because I was a different person then."

Lewis Carroll, Alice in Wonderland

"I can't keep this up." Francis gasped for air. With the help of Raziel and some of the Powers, they had sent thousands of demons back to Hell, but they were still coming.

"Rest," Raziel told him.

"I can't, more still come."

Raziel whistled in between thrashing his sword and three angels descended. "Don't let him die." Raziel motioned to Francis.

The angels surrounded Francis, giving him a moment to rest. He took a knee.

"Thank you, Raz," He panted.

"No prob--" Raziel stopped, his mouth wide.

The demons were scattering, and quickly.

"That can't be good." Francis stood.

"No." Raziel shook his head.

Raziel touched Francis and they Faded to the bedroom of Francis's apartment. Suriel and Jophiel stood there clearly confused. Vincent stood between them.

"They left Abditus, too, then?" Jophiel asked.

"Yes." Raziel confirmed.

298

Vincent stared at Francis for a long moment before hugging him. "Francis."

"Glad you're back, kid." Francis patted his back. "Now let's find your sister."

CHAPTER 34

"The journey of a thousand miles begins with a single step."
Lao Tzu

The car was spinning out of control as rain pelted the car. It was so thick they couldn't see anything, as if driving through a waterfall. Zeke had to throw his arm across Lilly's chest to hold her in place as the car screeched to a halt. His face was pale and terrified.

"Are you OK?"

"Yeah." She felt like her heart was going to pound right out of her chest and she was going to have to chase it down, but she was fine.

"It's Lex?"

"Yes." Zeke nodded.

Hovering his hands over the steering wheel Zeke began mumbling incoherently to himself. "Concentrate!" He snapped and hit the steering wheel hard with his fists. He looked up, one eye blue, one eye red. There was no emotion left on his face as he sped down the highway.

Before she could comment on his eyes there was a deafening screech. As fast as she could, Lilly flipped around in her seat to find where the noise was coming from. Through the rain were red beady eyes staring through the dark sky.

They were flying through the air as fast as the car, as if it were nothing.

The pedal slapped against the floor of the car and there was nothing more they could do. "He told them. He sold us out." Zeke's voice was cold and uncaring.

Lilly couldn't concentrate on anything as her wrists throbbed.

"It's no use now," Zeke said.

"But, it's almost time, the twenty-four hours is almost up." She winced.

"They'll catch us before that." His voice was grim.

"Zeke," the deep dying voice of Gahd called to him.

"Stay away, Gahd!" Zeke snapped.

"Make it easy on yourself, Zeke. Hand her over." Gahd flew next to the driver's side window. Her bony hand reached through the glass and clutched Zeke's shoulder.

"No."

"Just give her up. You'll be placed high up for handing her over." Gahd tilted her head to the side and grinned at Lilly.

Suddenly, Lilly's guardian angels appeared, one rested in the back seat and the other two flying, flanking the car.

Zeke thrust his hand out the window and grabbed Gahd by the throat. Gahd scratched at his arm furiously, but a jolt of blue light flew out of Zeke's hand and Gahd went crashing to the pavement.

The two flanking angels rose above the car with their swords drawn, prepared the fight the other demons. Most of the demons fell back a little, trying to decide how to move forward with their pursuit.

Zeke placed his hand on the dash again. The speedometer lost control and fell back to zero. The car jolted forward until the demons were out of sight.

Lilly clenched her eyes shut and pushed her head back into the seat, praying for the pain to stop. "I should have let her..."

"It's OK. Think of a happy moment."

Lilly nodded. She thought of her mom singing her to sleep, of the first time going to Abditus with Francis, then of the memory Sybil showed her. Eva holding her by her crib. She looked terrified, but it was a happy memory for Lilly being able to see her mother scoop her up from her crib. Her crib. Abditus. Her eyes shot open and she grabbed the locket on her neck. All three places shared the same Rune, ᛈ , Wunjo.

"It's in the woods," Lilly gasped.

The angel in the back seat perked up.

"What?"

"The Ferryman, the sword, it's in the woods."

The two other guardian angels reappeared, three of them now crammed in the back seat of Zeke's car. They leaned in towards Lilly.

"Get us to the park near school."

"Oregon Ridge?"

"Yes."

Zeke changed direction.

Her guardians disappeared.

Lilly called Francis. It only rang once before he answered.

"Are you OK?"

"There are demons on our heels, but I know where it is, I know where the sword is, Francis."

"Where are you now? Iris has been trying to find you for hours."

"Just south of I-83," Zeke chimed in.

"Iris is on her way."

"Meet us at the park, Francis."

"Yes." He hung up.

A few moments later Iris was there, but it was too late. Demons surrounded the car now that the guardians were gone; there was no way to escape them all without their own legion of angels.

"We'll have to trash the car." Iris put a hand on each of their shoulders.

"No." Zeke shook his head violently.

Iris took her hand off his shoulder. "Suit yourself."

"Fine!" Zeke grabbed Iris' arm.

"Picture the place," Iris told Lilly.

As soon as Lilly thought of the place in the woods, they were there in the woods.

Lilly imagined Zeke's car crashing into the median. As soon as the thought crossed her mind, it won her a look of rage from Zeke.

"Sorry…"

"Quick, we'll only have a few minutes before they realize where you've gone," Iris hastened them.

"OK, it was engraved on a tree, a Wunjo." Lilly held up her locket and showed them the rune on it. "It was about waist height."

They searched from tree to tree for the symbol.

"We'll never find it," Zeke said, distressed.

Iris stared at him shaking her head. "Keep looking."

"They're coming…" Zeke backed away. "I feel them, everywhere. It's too late, we're going to die."

"Calm yourself, Zeke," Iris snapped.

"It has to be here, it's where I pictured, it has to be the same place." Lilly took Sabriel from her belt and held it, steadily outstretched in her hand ready for any demons that emerged.

Dogs were barking and someone was running towards them.

"Francis," Iris nodded as he came running up to them.

"I can't stay, they'll kill me," Zeke said.

"Don't even think about leaving." Francis took Zeke by the shirt collar. "We die, you die." Francis spit at his feet.

"Francis, where is it?" Lilly asked.

"What?"

"Where we entered Abditus a while back? When we stepped directly into the coliseum. You acted as if it was a place you knew already."

"Because it is a place I know." Francis turned to his right. "There," he pointed.

Cuff and Link growled with their ears back flat; they were nothing but teeth. They faced out into the depths of the forest as the wind blew like a storm was near.

"There." Lilly reached out to the ᚹ carved into the tree. She touched it, but nothing happened. She touched it again. "I swore it would be here." Lilly's voice filled with panic, she pressed it harder.

"It is." Francis pointed to Sabriel, which was glowing bright as a full moon.

"Francis." Lilly motioned behind him.

Demons, more than she could count, soared towards them, dodging trees the whole way. Flapping wings and grinding teeth could be heard from all directions.

"The blade, touch the blade to it," Iris said.

As Lilly reached the blade towards it, the demons closed in. Iris and Francis stood around Lilly and the tree, swords drawn, while Zeke looked ready to collapse with fear.

No sooner did Lilly touch Sabriel's blade to the carved Þ and the tree trunk split unnaturally open. There, right before her, stood the Ferryman. It was nearly as tall as she was, covered in runes and vine-like engravings on the handle.

She handed Sabriel to Francis and used both hands to lift the Ferryman from the tree. It wasn't as heavy as it looked, but awkward, and its presence filled Lilly with a strange feeling: power.

The demons were all around them only feet away now, but they slowed at the sight of the sword. They looked back and forth between each other, unsure if they should continue.

Lilly fumbled with the sword in front of her and stared at the rows of demons. The others weren't sure what to do either. Then the demons parted and Gahd emerged from within them, grinning.

At the sight of Gahd, Zeke disappeared.

"Say it!" Francis bellowed. "Now!"

Lilly rested the tip of the sword on the ground in front of her and knelt, placing a hand on either side of the hilt. "With the power of this sword, I, Lilly, take authority as the new Keeper." She felt its power ripple through her and give her strength. Then she watched as it surged through the trees and everything around them, shaking the very ground they stood on.

Lilly lifted the sword as best she could.

"Go back to Hell!" She roared.

With her words every demon stopped completely, even Gahd. Some Faded right away, others lingered ready to challenge her. But Chamuel, Suriel, Jophiel, Gabriel, and Raziel appeared, encircling Lilly, Francis, and Iris.

"You heard her," Raziel commanded. "Leave now, or die."

The Archangels each held their own swords out in front of them ready to strike and took a step forward.

Some demons disappeared or ran, but the Archangels didn't give the closer ones a chance. Gabriel struck first. Gahd hung back, watching her demon companions fall before she disappeared.

CHAPTER 35

"I shall seize fate by the throat."

Ludwig van Beethoven

The last thing Lilly wanted to do now was go back to school. She wanted to find Zeke and teach him a lesson for leaving someone behind, or train as much as possible. The thought of sitting in a classroom with the Ferryman hidden away on her shoulder collecting dust while she had experienced the vastness of their demon problem firsthand made her sick. She had to do something.

Zeke hadn't tried to contact her and no one else had seen him since the incident, even at school.

Lilly looked over the cafeteria, half expecting to see him. Her friends laughed and talked about the upcoming winter break, but Lilly couldn't. Their contentment was false, if they only knew what lay just beyond their world, banging on their thin walls.

It was like the eye of the storm and Lilly wasn't going to be caught off guard and think it was over; the second wave would come. Zeke was out there somewhere, probably plotting how to kill her next.

"Hey, Lilly."

She jerked at the sound of the voice. It was Samael, looming over her like a cat ready to pounce. He was clean-shaven, wearing jeans and a t-shirt. He looked ten years younger. At his side lingered an unfamiliar female face.

Everyone at the table watched, confused by Samael and Lilly's interaction.

"What are you doing here?"

"Don't sound so surprised. We need our education too, you know," Samael winked.

"We enrolled this morning," the girl sighed as she scanned the cafeteria.

"This is Jaymie."

"Who are your friends, Lilly?" Quinn inquired from across the table.

"Oh, uh, Sam and Jaymie, they're--"

"Old friends from way back, today's our first day." The bell rang as Samael spoke.

"Mind showing me around, cowboy?" Jaymie asked Quinn.

Before Lilly had a chance to stop them, they were down the hall. Quinn couldn't take his eyes off Jaymie, who smiled back at Lilly, trying to torment her.

"Why are you here?" Lilly snapped.

"I've been reassigned since Zeke is AWOL."

Before Lilly could retort, Samael had his arm around Kathy and they were walking down the hall together.

She reached over her shoulder to the Ferryman with the intent to end them both, but her guardian appeared. "No," he said, brushing her hand away.

"Why can't I just kill him, Francis?" Lilly thrust the Ferryman into a practice dummy in Abditus.

"Samael checks out, he is contracted to the angel Zadkiel. He is at Wakefield to mend what Zeke has done." Jophiel said.

"I don't care, I don't trust him. Zeke said-"

"And Zeke could have been lying. We need to find out what we can, we can't just going around killing people, or Half Lives. Then we would be no better than demons, Lilly." Francis shook his head.

"He had Sybil." Lilly protested.

"He may have been protecting her, we don't know. It's all still very--" Jophiel was stopped mid sentence by Lilly.

"I won't wait around this time for Zeke or Samael or whoever to kill me," Lilly threatened, pointing the sword towards Jophiel, then Francis.

"And you won't go around killing for no reason." Francis lowered her sword.

"We'll help you uncover the truth." Suriel beamed. Excitedly, she dashed purple flowers here and there throughout the arena.

Jophiel grumbled, but didn't dare ask her to stop. Ever since their close run in she hadn't let anyone tell her she couldn't make the entire world purple if she liked. Chamuel even broke a smile seeing all the purple, but only for a moment.

"Then I'll be ready when one of them slips up." Lilly uttered and thrust the Ferryman into the dummy once more.

"Of course you will, Miho," Francis chuckled.

Gabriel landed out of breath, holding Raziel up. Everyone held still. Gabriel let go and Raziel fell to the purple ground of the arena, unmoving, blood dripping from his head and chest. Gabriel fell to his knees and stared straight at Lilly.

"What's happened?" Jophiel stood.

"Someone has opened the second gate of Hell," Gabriel uttered before collapsing next to Raziel.

About the Author

'The Half Life' is the debut novel from Ellie Elisabeth, a 2010 Electronic Media and Film graduate from Towson University. At age 22 Ellie became her own boss and started a dog grooming business called Snazzy Jazzy's, named for her first dog Jasper. She currently lives in Maryland with her husband Shaun, three dogs, cats, reptiles, and ever-growing *zoo*.

For more information about
Ellie Elisabeth, upcoming releases,
The Legacy of Lilly Guthrie Series,
story companion, & contest go to:

www.EllieElisabeth.com

Acknowledgements

Thank you to everyone who took the time to read and critique the beginnings of this seven book series.

Thank you to my amazing husband, Shaun, for never doubting me, always encouraging me, and putting up with my eccentricities.

To my incredible family: Dad, Ruth, Zach, and Jessica who without a doubt have always been there for me through thick and thin.

To my nephew, Matthew, who has always been my biggest fan and greatest critic. The world can expect great things from you.

To my friends who never doubted me: Brittany, Barbara, Courtney, Liz, Maria, and Sarah.

To Andrew, Betsy, Gina, Mandy, and Eric who have taught me much more than they will ever know about life, love, hard work, and believing in myself.

To everyone who has showed kindness and reminded me that there is light at the end of the tunnel.

Thank you Mom. Your presence is never forgotten.

And to Jasper, Gideon, and Daryl who always provide listening ears to any silly thing I consider putting on paper.

75590732R00191

Made in the USA
Columbia, SC
23 August 2017